Minutes to Live

STEPHANIE FLYNN

Small Fish Publishing
USA

First edition
Cover design by Stephanie Flynn

ISBN eBook: 9781952372001
ISBN paperback: 9781952372490
ISBN hardcover: 9781952372728
ISBN large print: 9781952372735

Special Note

Time travel is real.
For a few short hours, you will be transported
to 1987 and back again.
Enjoy the ride.

NOTE: Minutes to Live is the prequel to Matchmaker in Time, a time travel romance series, and the time travel begins at the end of this story. This is the only book in the series with NO HEA. Kiko gets hers in book 4. This can be read at any point before book 4, Years to Savor.

Chapter 1

1987, Milwaukee, Wisconsin

THE SOONER KIKO HADA memorized all the content in front of her and breezed through the rest of her college classes, the sooner she could escape. A pencil shimmied between her fingertips, and her brows knitted in concentration. A brick of a textbook, split open on her paisley bedspread, rested before her, and with her feet up in the air, Kiko blew bubbles with her chewing gum. Every twenty minutes or so, she'd shift the book's position on her bed so the sunlight coming in through the window wouldn't reflect off the page and burn her retinas. She'd been studying all day and still she had so far to go.

Downstairs, the front door slammed shut, rattling the walls and startling her. Now Mom and Dad were home, and that meant peaceful study time was over.

The television downstairs blared a roaring football audience and an obnoxious commentator. Dad was becoming one with the recliner. Kiko turned the page as a plate crashed on the kitchen linoleum. Dad shouted. Mom yelled for help in the kitchen, triggering the same old argument—who worked more hours, who did more chores, who should get a break from cooking dinner. If Kiko recorded a fight like today's and played it when her parents got home, they would save so much energy.

With a few exceptions, Kiko saved every penny she earned to cover the difference after scholarships, and damned if she would lose her opportunity to finish school because her parents wouldn't stop fighting. October in Wisconsin wasn't conducive to studying outside, and after her closing shift at the Gap and waiting for public transit, the library closed too early to bother. Kiko's eyes roamed her sparse walls, seeking comfort from bright cornflower blue eyes and a crooked grin. The Michael J. Fox poster, her favorite after seeing *Back to the Future* in the theater recently, watched over her every night. "Pretty soon, Mr. Fox, we'll get out of here."

With a growling stomach and screaming parents, Kiko blew out a deep breath and shut her book. Quantitative and qualitative research methods had to take a break. Was there any possible way she could scrape together the funds to move out? Kiko snorted to herself. Only in a fantasy world.

With years of practice, Kiko kept quiet as she climbed downstairs to prevent the fight from redirecting at her. In the kitchen, Mom swept up porcelain plate shards with tears in her eyes. In the living room, Dad had turned the volume up on the television. It was almost unbearable. The neighbors must've hated their fights almost as much as she did. Kiko stepped over to the coffee table, careful to stay out of Dad's view, and she collected the newspaper and tucked it under her arm.

"What do you want with that?" Dad asked.

Kiko flinched. "Um, essay for school," she lied.

Dad grunted in disinterest, and Kiko slinked over to the kitchen and squatted by the mess. She whispered, "Need any help in here?" Kiko picked up larger shards and placed them onto the dustpan.

"No." Mom's voice was clipped.

Kiko was used to being brushed aside, but that didn't stop her from trying to support her mom. Their household hadn't always been so strained. After Dad's work hours were reduced a few years ago, the paychecks shrank. But that wasn't the only problem, nor the real reason for the fights. Even with less working hours, Dad stayed out just as long, sometimes longer. Neither of her parents ever had a straightforward conversation about it—the proverbial elephant in the room. At least, not around Kiko.

Kiko knew her place. Since high school graduation, she and her parents had an agreement: As long as Kiko remained a student, she didn't pay rent, but she bought her own groceries.

Having helped as much as she could with bare hands, Kiko stood and rummaged in her supply of food. She opened a foil pack of Pop-Tarts, and dropped both pastries into the toaster, because dinner didn't include her unless she specified ahead of time. Mom's cooking wasn't the best, and the discomfort at the dinner table wasn't worth it. Kiko leaned against the counter and waited for her dinner.

Mom emptied the dustpan into the trash, but it slipped from her fingers, falling to the floor. In a fit of frustration, she picked up the dustpan and threw it into the trash too. She slammed the lid three times to get it to close and growled in anger.

Kiko winced and lifted her hot pastries, passing them back and forth so her hands didn't burn, and brought them up to her room. She plopped onto her bedspread, laid out the newspaper, and took a bite of steaming strawberry pastry.

It was time to find an apartment of her own, even if she couldn't afford furniture. A roof, quiet, and food were all she needed to finish school. The first ad she read felt like it was written for her.

> Your home no longer your sanctuary? Find
> your inner peace with me. For all your
> purchasing and renting needs, call real estate
> agent Kiyoshi Takai today!

That evening, Kiko waited until Dad was asleep on the recliner and Mom was in the shower. She padded down the stairs to the kitchen phone and dialed the number for the agent. With the long curly cord, she stepped around the corner into the laundry room. She didn't want to wake Dad with her call.

"Hello?" a groggy youthful man answered. Kiko's stomach fluttered at his sensual voice.

"I'm sorry, I hope it's not too late to disturb you. Is this Kiyoshi Takai from the newspaper ad?"

The man cleared his throat and instantly perked up. "You got him. Anything you need, I can find. So tell me, what can I do for you?"

Her voice was hushed, as if discussing a secret scandalous getaway, and pulses of excitement rushed through her. "I need an apartment, but it has to be quiet and very cheap. Can you help me?"

"Absolutely. Saturday at lunch? I can show you the available properties."

"I can do that. Where do we meet?" Kiko's heart thundered in her ears.

"Drop by my office." He recited the address, and Kiko repeated it in her head half a dozen times to remember it.

"Can I get your name?"

Kiko wanted to be taken seriously, so she gave him the serious version of her name. "Ms. Hada."

I'll see you then, Ms. Hada," he said. The call disconnected in her hand.

Dad's snoring stopped. Kiko froze and waited. With his shifting weight, the springs of the recliner protested, but after a beat, the snoring resumed. The thought of waking him made her shudder.

Kiko stared at the phone in amazement. Just like that, the sensuous disembodied voice of Kiyoshi Takai promised to liberate her from her parents. A wave of energy pulsed in her bones at the thrill of pending independence, which sounded completely insane, but for the first time in her life, she'd have peace and privacy. She smiled at the phone and replaced it on the cradle with care to minimize the clatter.

Kiko padded back up stairs and slipped into her room just as Mom turned off the water in the shower. Kiko didn't want to answer questions tonight.

Inside the cover of her *Research Methods in Psychology* textbook, she scribbled the address and stuffed the book inside her backpack. This invisible stranger was already her savior and he didn't even know it.

Sleep wouldn't come with her thoughts bouncing from making her own meals to having a private bathroom and studying without distractions. It would be so serene—a magical fairy tale come true. Kiko turned on her lamp, brought her textbook back out, and took advantage of the quiet.

Chapter 2

Freshly washed with a towel hanging at the nape of his neck after kendo class, Kiyoshi Takai held open the dojo's door. His classmate and friend Roger Meyer, always accompanied him out. While Kiyoshi hit the bus stop, Roger headed for the parking garage. The crisp autumn air sent goosebumps up Kiyoshi's arms, but after the pulse-pounding sparring and a hot shower, he didn't feel the chill.

As Kiyoshi introduced Roger to kendo, Roger had introduced him to real estate, and since Kiyoshi was flat broke before, he was grateful for the job. That was where their similarities ended. The large, broad shouldered man, who better fit the profile of a football player, was the epitome of fashion with suits in a range of colors, fluffy blond hair, and designer shades. He was a decent guy if one avoided conversations about money or women, which was sometimes difficult. Kiyoshi would never admit that he was envious of Roger's lucky fortune with the ladies. But where his friend enjoyed a steady stream of women, Kiyoshi just wanted one. It wasn't his smooth-shaven mug—he received plenty of initial attention—but they never stuck around. Hopefully now that he had a job, Kiyoshi might just get lucky too.

"Commercial is where the money is, man," Roger said.

"Residential is where the women are." Even if most of them were married.

Roger laughed. "And your luck with that so far has been...?"

"Zilch." Kiyoshi smiled at his own expense, and a gusty breeze cooled him through his light T-shirt.

"I figured. You've only been in the position for a few months. Hang in there. Besides, what are you losing? Oh, just money."

Kiyoshi pressed his lips together in frustration. He preferred working residential real estate. The odds of meeting a woman were higher in residential, but that was not the real reason he preferred the lower-paying department. Every time he helped a family find a house they could call home, it lit a warm glow in his chest. The excitement on their faces when they stepped inside 'the one' kept him smiling for days. Roger was right—his paycheck didn't compete, but there was more to life than a fat wallet.

"What was up at kendo today? You missed parries. You let Woodson take points on you," Roger said.

Kiyoshi set his bag down on the bus stop bench. "In my defense, Eric Woodson is a competent fighter. If you weren't such a lumbering giant, I'd wager he'd be better than you."

Before Roger could rub in the pseudo compliment, Eric appeared and bopped Kiyoshi on the back of the head with his gear bag while walking by. "At least you know your place, pal," Eric said with a friendly insult.

"Beat it, Woodson. You won't get so lucky tomorrow," Kiyoshi retorted.

"Wanna bet?"

Kiyoshi laughed to hide his crying wallet. "Maybe next time."

Eric and Roger were similar in many ways. Both were tall and blond and came from money. But Eric was lean like Kiyoshi. Eric continued down toward the parking garage and swung his arm in a wave goodbye. Lucky bastard had a car, like Roger. They were both great fighters too, but Eric was always fair, while Roger would cheat if he found an opening. Thankfully, Roger used his bulk and didn't need to skirt the rules often. Eric Woodson was good people. Roger...depended on the day.

"You think there's a chance he could ever beat me?" Roger asked, studying the shrinking shape of Eric as if considering changing his routine opponents. Their dojo split the students into different weight classes during training for the safety of the little kids, but sparring was a free-for-all. Roger chose opponents of similar size, which didn't include Kiyoshi or Eric.

Kiyoshi shrugged. He didn't want to see that fight. Roger had a temper no one should cross.

Eric disappeared into the parking garage, and Roger asked, "So, what's the excuse for sucking against Woodson today?" He nudged Kiyoshi on the shoulder.

"I got a call late last night. I've got a showing Saturday."

"That's all it takes to throw you off your game?" Roger asked with an arch to his brow.

"The woman had a voice like an angel. I can just picture what she looks like." Kiyoshi made an hourglass shape with his hands for his friend's amusement. Her voice was trapped in Kiyoshi's head all day.

"Hey, that's great news." Roger stuffed a finger inside a small hole in Kiyoshi's shirt seam. "Commission can't come soon enough. Put on something extra nice. Fake it 'til you make it. Push her into the nicest place in your portfolio."

"I'll give the client the best match I can find."

"And that's why you don't have money. Where are you off to now?" Roger asked and pointed at the bus stop bench.

"Back to the office."

"What about lunch?"

"That was lunch," Kiyoshi said. Rigorous activity helped ease the hunger pangs.

"Oh, nonsense. You just worked up an appetite. I never see you eat. Let's get some sushi." Roger dangled his car keys in an offer to drive.

"How about sushi delivered to the office?" Kiyoshi always prioritized kendo, the only link he knew to his heritage. His next priority was finding real estate leads to make rent, and going out to lunch not only wasted time but further drained his wallet.

"Sure, man," Roger said.

Kiyoshi hefted his equipment bag back onto his shoulder, and the pair of them strolled toward the parking garage. Roger used his monstrous shoe of a phone, a state-of-the-art piece of equipment Roger called a 'cellular telephone', to order delivery to the office.

The glass building towered among other downtown office structures. Kiyoshi craned his neck and wondered who had the penthouse floor. Someday it would be Roger's, he guessed. By the time they entered the front doors, steaming bags of rice with mouth-watering sushi awaited them on the welcome desk. Behind which, Doris the secretary, both plenty gray and plump, sat with a cigarette dangling out of her lips, typing on her boxy computer. Their footsteps echoed in the expansive foyer with tile floors and large palm plants. The lacquered honey brown paneling behind her reflected her computer screen with a glowing blue rectangle.

"Doris, my dear, did you pay the delivery driver?" Roger asked with a flirty tone and leaned an elbow on the counter.

"Yes, sir," she mumbled without dropping her cigarette.

"How much?" Roger fished in his back pocket and retrieved an envious stack of folded twenties fastened with a silver clip.

"Twelve dollars, sir."

Roger flipped through the stack and dropped a twenty onto the desk in front of her. "Thanks, honey."

She blushed with a sheepish grin, tapped off her ash, and pocketed the money. They exchanged winks, and Roger collected the bags of food.

Inside the elevator, Kiyoshi said with suggestive inflection, "So, uh, you and Doris?"

"Doris and I what?"

Kiyoshi made awkward gestures to show the two of them were together. "You know, seeing each other?"

Roger laughed. "No way. Why would you think that?"

"Oh, never mind." Kiyoshi shook his head. So far, Roger never got into trouble with all those uninhibited relations.

There must've been some miracle worker on his shoulder, or he traded his soul for his good fortune. Both options were equally likely.

"I got me a girl, Yoshi. Jessica is the sexiest thing I've touched."

"You could've fooled me." Kiyoshi beamed, happy for his friend while surprised someone tamed Roger. "Since when?"

"Couple weeks ago."

Kiyoshi ribbed his friend with a nudge to his shoulder. "That's great. Why haven't you told me?"

His friend shrugged. "At first it was just another fling. Nothing worth mentioning. But something kept me going back for more, and not just her nice rack either. Something that just made me crazy for her, you know?"

Kiyoshi didn't. He'd had girlfriends, but nothing serious. Once they saw his rented house, they ran for the hills. Sure, he wasn't rich like Roger, but it wasn't like he had cockroaches or anything. One day he hoped to have that passionate, animalistic desire for a woman, and more importantly—that she lusted for him too.

The elevator dinged at the fourth floor. Main Street Realty didn't follow the current 80s trends like the building's owner displayed at the ground floor. No, MSR was stuck squarely in 1970. Walls were thin wood paneling, and cubicles in neat rows sat on lime green carpet. The orange-accented desks thankfully had a computer terminal humming on each one, so no more writing out documents by hand. Private offices, where Roger parked his rear during the day, ran the perimeter. Kiyoshi led Roger down the aisle, set his equipment bag underneath his desk, and collected his sushi from his friend.

"How much do I owe you?"

"Don't worry about it." Roger patted him on the back and pivoted on his heels.

"Hey, Rodg, want to rent a flick tonight?"

His friend chuckled. "Nah, man. I'm busy." He wagged his brows and strolled to his private office. Roger's father owned the company, and at the ripe old age of twenty-six, Roger had his own private office with a view. Kiyoshi was only a few years younger, but Roger treated him like a little brother sometimes. Kiyoshi was only a few years younger, but Roger treated him like a little brother sometimes. When he and Roger had clicked at the dojo, his friend offered him a job at his dad's company. To Kiyoshi, it was a winning lottery ticket, so he performed his best to not screw it up.

Kiyoshi's answering machine read no missed messages, so he unwrapped a sushi roll. He inhaled the first four and then opened a search engine on his terminal.

Since the age of five, he'd known he was different. When he turned ten, his parents told him the truth: they adopted him. His parents raised him in the suburbs, where he was the only Japanese boy in school. His parents explained it was a closed adoption, and they couldn't tell him anything about his birth parents.

He searched census records each week for clues to his origins, and anytime he had a lead, he filed paperwork with the clerk of courts in that county. He feared his birth parents had died or that they would be furious with a reunion. Kiyoshi wouldn't even know what to say. Perhaps he only needed a name to fill in that missing piece in his heart.

Chapter 3

AT THE PROSPECT OF freedom, Kiko hadn't been able to concentrate, and by Friday night, she needed a break from the books. So on a very rare night off, she planned to enjoy herself without guilt. *Indiana Jones and the Temple of Doom* had been hyped up for the last year, and Kiko needed to finally see it, so she rode the bus to Blockbuster to rent the movie.

Light blazed out of the windows like a UFO parked in a darkened lot. Inside, rapid gunfire and yelling echoed from the massive screen on the back wall airing a new release. Video escapes lined the walls and rows upon rows of floor shelving units. She dragged her finger along a shelf while she skimmed each box in the older releases section.

A fellow customer, busy reading the back of a movie case, caught her attention. He had shiny raven hair, a smooth angular jaw, and the lean frame of a model. He dressed in a striped button up, opened at his throat, and black dress pants. That model belonged on Tiger Beat magazine. His head turned in her direction as if hearing her thoughts, and she ducked behind the shelf, face burning hot in embarrassment.

Kiko needed an excuse for hiding, just in case he busted her. Emergency loose laces on aisle six! That'll do. Kiko shook her head at the silliness and stood up. Her eyes sought the model again. No harm in looking, she thought.

He stood right in front of her on the other side of the shelf, reading another cover. Heat flashed up her throat and face again. She tried to focus on the video cases, but her brain didn't register the words in front of her.

Kiko walked down the aisle away from him, flustered like a high school girl. She released a deep breath to steady herself and find her movie. It was released last year, so it wouldn't be buried in the older movie section. She stopped and steeled herself, realizing she needed to pass by him again. When she turned around, he was gone. She sought him out while she wiped her sweaty palms on her jeans. Strangely disappointed, she resumed her perimeter search for Indiana Jones.

Right around the corner, the model stood blocking her way. Startled, she blurted, "Oh, hi! I didn't see you there." The so-beautiful-it-should-be-illegal model's head turned. His captivating light brown eyes matched a latte that's had too much milk. His lips parted just a fraction while his eyes drank her in.

With her brain misfiring on what must've been a misinterpretation of his hot gaze, she noticed the movie in his hand. *Indiana Jones and the Temple of Doom*. She checked the wall in front of him, and all the remaining cases on the shelf had no VHS tape behind them. In his hands was the last copy. Her heart hammered in her chest, but her brain formed the connection to her tongue. "Were you going to rent that? I came for that movie."

The model stammered and glanced down at the movie in his hands. "Oh, uh, yeah." After a second, he smiled deviously. "I've been waiting all year for this one. It's a bummer they only have one copy left."

His voice made her melt, but she stood firm in her plans for the evening. "Do you mind letting me rent it first? I've been wanting to see it too."

The model leaned against the shelf with a casual confidence radiating off him. "How about we rent it together?"

The word 'together' surprised her. Did he want a date? "I...I live with my parents," she said, disappointed once again in her living situation.

"Well, I don't. We can watch this at my place, and no one will care how loud we play it, not even the neighbors."

This was a difficult conundrum—not. Go to her parents' house empty handed and listen to them yelling, or watch a movie with a smoking hot guy. She didn't want to appear desperate for a single night of fun though, and she didn't want to appear easy. "I don't think that's such a great idea," she said without conviction.

"I tell you what. We can order pizza delivery."

No way would she reject dinner and a movie with a sexy model—a trifecta of perfection. Besides, a broke college student would never turn down pizza.

"With mushrooms, onions, and olives?" Her playful tone already told him her answer.

"Perhaps"—he tapped his chin with his index finger—"but as a carnivore myself, I insist on pepperoni." His eyes flashed with mischievousness.

"I think I can work with that."

"Fantastic. You cover the movie, and I'll cover the grub?" He held out the movie to her. Either way, it was hers now. She smiled.

"Deal."

They went to the checkout, and she told the clerk the phone number to her account. "There's a one-dollar fee if you forget to rewind," the clerk reminded her.

"Yes, thank you."

Kiko stepped outside into the darkness, and her skin crackled with an awareness of the model's presence next to her. Cones of orange light bathed the parking lot. A sprinkle of cars parked before them. Kiko wondered which was his, if any. "Do you have a car?" she asked. His face fell. A car would be convenient, but she didn't care either way.

He rubbed the back of his neck. "I take the bus. You?"

"Bus for me, too." They exchanged smiles and caught the next bus together. While the wheels hummed on the pavement, butterflies in her stomach played the game of tag. She said, "I didn't get your name."

"My friends call me Yoshi."

"I'm Kiko."

"Nice to meet you," he said, holding out his hand.

She shook it and laughed. "Assume nothing." He quirked a brow at her, and she continued, "I'm just saying you don't know me, so you may decide it wasn't nice to meet me after all."

"Well, we can fix that." His eyes narrowed with a glint of challenge. "What do you do for a living?"

She chuckled at his game. "I work at the Gap during the day and most weekends. But I'm in school."

"What for?"

Kiko cringed. She valued education above all else. "So I don't have to work retail for the rest of my life." That should've been obvious.

Yoshi's velvety laugh calmed the haywire nerves in her belly. "I mean, what's your major?"

Kiko held her chin up. "Psychology."

"A shrink, huh? What made you choose that?"

"Not a shrink." She folded her arms over her chest. "I'll be a marriage and family counselor. From personal experience, it appears to be a very necessary profession."

"You look a little young to be having marital problems." Now he was sassy. It irritated her, but yet felt liberating to speak with someone who wasn't in her normal social circle, which consisted of clueless classmates, dull customers, and fighting parents.

"I'm not married, and you need a little tact."

"Sorry. I didn't expect heavy topics"—he checked his watch—"twenty minutes into meeting someone."

"Well, my choice of schooling is personal. My parents fight. A lot. I want to help families stay together and function. I want to help, so their kids aren't hearing..." she trailed off. She picked at the hard plastic edge of the rental tape.

"I'm sorry you have to listen to that. It's a shame that two adults can't calmly discuss their differences and solve them as a team."

Impressed with his level of maturity and insight, Kiko's head whipped back to him. "You sound like you have experience."

Yoshi sighed. "I was teased relentlessly as a kid, because I was different than my parents and most of my school. I snapped one day. After I got in trouble, I accused my parents of stealing me, and I threatened to call the cops. My parents finally sat me down and explained they adopted me. But when they told me, they were calm and collected. I had a few outbursts trying to understand, but I would've been a runaway if they weren't so supportive of my feelings. In fact, they are great parents. They even supported me quitting school."

"You quit? Why? What are you doing?" Kiko couldn't fathom how anyone gave up their future voluntarily—unless...he was a wicked-rich model.

"I majored in general studies because I didn't know what I wanted to do with my life, and I didn't want to have regrets. My friend Roger, from my dojo, got me a job at his dad's real estate company. So now I sell real estate."

"Oh, that's different."

"Disappointed?"

She wasn't disappointed in a stranger's career, but it was a career path she hadn't considered. Since childhood, she'd only ever dreamed of becoming a therapist to help people. To skip school altogether was a foreign concept.

"No. It's just that I never met anyone successful without college."

He fidgeted in his seat. The bus pulled up to the curb, and he jumped to his feet. "Here's our stop."

Kiko followed him off the bus and gazed at the darkened house. One window was broken, one was boarded, and no lights were on. "Is this your place?" she asked with dread. Suddenly going to a strange man's home late at night seemed like a terrible idea.

"This one is me," he said, nodding to the corner house next door. Yoshi's house was next to the murder house. She wasn't sure how much better that was. Relief rolled through her anyway, and they walked toward a light blue house with overgrown shrubs, no broken windows, and a night light that showed signs of life.

Chapter 4

THE JAGGED SIDEWALK TO Kiyoshi's house was composed of raised and tilted concrete squares, and in the dark with a broken streetlight on the corner, it was hard to see. After living here for two years, Kiyoshi took confident steps. Kiko wasn't as lucky. She tripped on a raised seam, and he caught her by the hand. A touch of her warm, soft skin jolted through his body, wakening him like never before. Kiko challenged him and was a deadly combination of smart as hell and stunning. A long curtain of midnight hair hung down her back, her dark eyes were like gazing into the night sky, and she had the perfect lithe shape to fit into his lean frame. He hoped he got a chance to feel her body against his. It had been far too long since he'd brought someone home.

She smiled, brightening her face, and Kiyoshi was ever so grateful Kiko had found him at Blockbuster.

"I got you," he said.

Bummer she still lived with her parents. At least they had his place, and fingers crossed she didn't run away screaming when she saw the inside. He wasn't a slob or anything. It's just his landlord charged low rent for a reason. He would treat her like a queen for however long he was with her, which he suspected would be about ten more minutes.

Kiyoshi brought her inside while worry filled his chest. When he'd brought Kristen here a few months ago, the grimace on her face was telling, and no matter how much food or drink he offered her, or how much he tried seducing her, she made an excuse about leaving the oven on, and she left in a hurry. Gone before he even had a chance. He hoped Kiko could see beyond his house, and now it was time for the verdict. Please, please, please, he silently begged her to stay. Exhaling a deep breath, he flicked on the lights.

"Whoa," she said with surprise and awe.

He owned only one thing worthy of that response: his prized katana displayed above the fireplace mantle. His heart sped in excitement. She didn't run away screaming, and his authentic Japanese steel impressed her. Maybe that was what chased Kristen away. If so, then she wasn't the right one for him.

"You like it?" He encouraged conversation about it any chance he found. Roger never cared about its significance, only that it was a sharp, shiny hunk of metal meant to slice and dice. And since Kiyoshi wouldn't let Roger play with it, the blond brute lost interest.

"It's different. It looks old."

Kiyoshi thought 'different' meant something good. He beamed with pride and accepted the opportunity. He stepped over to his sword and removed it from its display.

"You're right, it's old and authentic. Been in my family for centuries," he said.

Her face scrunched in confusion, and he remembered he told her he was adopted.

"Or so the story goes," he added. Someone who claimed to be my great-grandfather handed my adoptive parents this sword. He said it rightfully belonged to me, and the old man was passing it down to the next generation. And, if anyone showed up demanding the return of it, to refuse. My parents never got his name, and they never heard from him again."

He unsheathed the blade, and Kiko backed up a step. Her eyes darted to the front door.

Slow down, chum, too much too fast. "I won't hurt you. I would never hurt you. This sword I treat like a piece of art. Beautiful, serious, delicate." He tilted it into the overhead light, and it reflected like a mirror.

Kiko leaned over the blade and admired it. A dainty finger traced a pattern on the hilt and touched the edge of the blade in a test. "It's still sharp."

"It's Japanese steel. It'll be sharp forever."

She scrunched her nose again in disbelief. "I can think of a few things that might dull its shine."

"Well, yeah, if someone runs it over with a Mack truck wearing snow chains," he said.

She laughed, a sweet melody to his ears. "I'm glad no one has, yet. It's beautiful, and I wonder, throughout the centuries, everything this blade has seen. Can you imagine? Horses and buggies? Cannon fire in war? Steamboats? What would it feel like back then with no power lines, no streetlights, no gas-guzzling machines roaring down roads?" Her fingers stroked the sword again, this time in admiration.

Kiyoshi had never been in love. He never believed in love at first sight, but after that line, his confidence wavered. Lust and desire pulsed through him. He wanted to get her on the couch, so he had an excuse to touch her.

"Thank you," he whispered. Kiyoshi's head swam with affection, having someone respect something that meant so much to him.

"Uh, you're welcome?"

Unable to explain his embarrassing awe, Kiyoshi's cheeks heated in a flush, and now it was time for a change of subject. "Let me get the pizza ordered." Kiyoshi zipped over to his phone and dialed the memorized number to the local pizza shop. Most days he could stretch the fourteen inch into three meals. Tonight that wasn't going to happen, but he had no regrets.

Kiyoshi watched her out of the corner of his eye while he placed the order. She strolled around his house, more curious than disgusted. The exterior of his house left much to be desired, and the interior wasn't much better. On his budget, he only wanted warm and quiet, so he'd only bought the bare necessities to fill the empty space. From a second-hand store, he'd scrounged up a mismatched collection of plain furniture, since he worried more about putting food in the fridge than coordinating patterns on the fabric. The walls were empty—no art, posters, or photographs, not that the landlord would notice any nail holes with all the cracks and patches in the drywall—and the counters and flooring hadn't been updated in decades. It wasn't much, but it was his.

Kiko opened the hard plastic case on the rental tape, and she bent over, her fingers making quick work of the VHS player and his big screen television. Since the weekly NFL game was his primary home entertainment, he'd splurged on a screen half the size of a refrigerator for that purpose. She popped in the movie and parked herself on the couch. After a few seconds of learning the remote-control buttons, she started up and paused the movie.

Kiyoshi hung up the phone. "Should we start it now or wait until after the food gets here?"

Kiko checked her watch. "Forty minutes for the pizza, right?"

"Thereabouts."

"We can start it and take a break when it gets here." She patted the couch cushion next to her.

Kiyoshi's breaths hitched. She wouldn't have to ask twice. He flew to her side. With a press of a button, the movie restarted. How was he going to focus on the flick with a woman sitting next to him who smelled like tropical flowers? His palms were sweating. He was rusty in the art of seduction, but he took the plunge with the old yawn-and-reach-around move to see if she would lean into him.

She did.

Chapter 5

Focusing on the movie proved to be difficult. To Kiko, Yoshi's house was heaven. Sure, it had a vintage style interior, peeling paint, loose carpet, and the kitchen linoleum had a wear path. There was hardly any furniture, and it smelled like stale fabric. But it was his own. A place to do what he wanted, when he wanted, and what made her envious—he had peace and quiet. It stood on a corner, and the neighboring murder-like house was empty. He had nothing to be ashamed of. Kiko was completely jealous.

The sword was the only thing of note in this house, and she liked it because it was unusual but oddly familiar, and she also liked it because it inspired passion in Yoshi. Kiko had broken up with her last boyfriend over two years ago, and that missing need grew with Kiyoshi's body pressed alongside hers. Under her clothes, her skin tingled with a pleading desire. And she was fully aware of his arm inching closer to her shoulder. She hid her amusement at his being too shy to just go for it. Soon she'd have her own home just like this, and the surge of independence and relief made her feel invincible, like she could do anything. On her one night off, she knew exactly what she wanted to do.

Even though the movie was amazing so far, they had a two-day rental period, so she could watch it herself tomorrow night—er, she couldn't take another night off from her studies. Kiko would just re-rent it another time then. She tilted her head toward Yoshi's exceptionally shaped jaw. "Kiss me," she whispered.

Yoshi startled. "What?"

Kiko smiled. It hadn't dawned on her until now that he might not have much experience. Well, she would fix that. "Kiss me," she repeated.

As if she'd flipped a light switch, Yoshi crushed his lips against hers. Their mouths explored each other, and his hands cupped her neck. Warmth charged her pulse and poured from her fingers to her toes, pooling just where she wanted it. The throbbing culminated between her legs, and she shifted to straddle his lap. A bulge grew underneath her, and fire burned in her body knowing he wanted her. Kiko pulled her lips away for a second, his breaths puffing against her face.

"Need help with that?" she asked playfully.

"If you're offering assistance, I won't turn you down." He rumbled with lust and dug in his pocket for a foil packet. Between two fingers, he pinched a condom.

Kiko opened the condom, unzipped his fly, and released him. A stiff erection popped out before her, and Kiko's eyes widened.

Yoshi chuckled at her reaction. "Everything all right?" he asked.

He wasn't huge, and he wasn't tiny. His size was the perfect fit to grind against. After Kiko shook off the pleasant surprise, she smiled deviously and rolled the condom on. "It will be."

Yoshi's head fell back and the hard length bobbed in her hands. Wrapped and ready to go, Yoshi lifted Kiko off his lap and set her next to him. He rose from the couch, dress pants pooling at his ankles. Yoshi kneeled at the couch and growled, "Mind if I go first?"

Kiko's pulse pounded while her hands scrambled to unbutton her acid-wash jeans. She lifted her hips right to his face. Yoshi tugged both jeans and underwear off with a smooth slip of his wrists and flung them aside. Strong hands caressed her body, exploring every tingling inch of her skin. He quickly found her small breasts, and his lips curved in an appreciative smile. Kiko relaxed because he didn't judge her lack of curves.

Yoshi unclasped her bra with a single hand, and she leaned forward for him to toss her remaining clothes aside. Exposed to the cool air, her nipples begged for the warm attention of his tongue. As if they were a beacon activated for him only, soft lips took her in and a wet tongue flicked. He sucked and teased her sensitive skin, and she writhed under him. With his mouth busy, Yoshi's fingers found her exposed entrance, and she gasped upon penetration. She gripped his thick hair to ground herself.

Yoshi touched and explored, first sliding in and out slowly until his fingers were wet. "Don't stop," she begged with a soft whimper. Using slick fingers, Yoshi rubbed her throbbing clit, and Kiko moaned. The fiery sizzle coursing through her bones charged her like a wild animal, desperate to join bodies. He moved faster, and a heat built in her core, driving her to gyrate against him.

A warm rush shot through her, tensing every muscle in her body, and she held her breath through the climax. As she spilled over, she cried out, "Yoshi! Oh god, Yoshi." The man knew how to find the clit. Kiko hadn't guessed at first. He rubbed and circled with his fingers, allowing her to ride out the waves of aftershocks.

Yoshi grinned. "You like that?"

"You know it. Now it's my turn." She pushed him away from her and stood. He was much too big for her to lift and flip around like he'd done to her. With a stern pointing finger, she ordered him onto the couch.

Yoshi, with a satisfied grin on his lips and a fiery hunger on his hooded lids, sat on the couch, knees spread wide for her with his pants locking his ankles.

Kiko loved being in charge. The ability to make a man turn to mush and lose control using her hands and mouth intoxicated her. She loved every moment.

KIYOSHI'S ERECTION THROBBED AND bounced with anticipation, and his belly swirled with liquid heat. Her hands unbuttoned his shirt with the speed and efficiency of an unknown ticking clock, but he didn't want her to slow down. Kiko splayed her hands on his bare chest, exploring the defined crevices of his abs, his rounded pecs, and nipples begging for attention. She pinched and rubbed, and he understood she did it for her own pleasure as much as his, and that was sexy as hell.

His body roared hot as an engine, begging with a primal urge to please her until her hips became numb. The smokiness in her eyes told him she was feral in the sheets, and he only prayed he would get the chance to see her fully in action. Holding her eye contact, she kissed, nipped, and sucked her way down his chest. A low rumble escaped his throat as her tongue flicked through the ridges of his abs and circled down to his inner thighs.

She was good. His wrapped erection bobbed in agreement. And finally, the main show began. Kiko took his head in her mouth, flicking her tongue against his opening. Her lips formed a suction seal, and he moaned. Kiko gathered spit and lathered his shaft. With her hands she stroked him while her tongue danced around his sensitive head and dipped low. Nerves sparked throughout his body, and heat accumulated along his length. "Oh god, that's so good. You are amazing."

She kneaded his balls, and they clenched.

"Kiko, you're making me come. I'm going to come."

She didn't stop or slow down. His breath hitched, and he growled out, "Kiko, right now!" She kept sucking and bobbing her head as he spilled over, filling the condom.

Kiko stopped, and the doorbell rang, and both their heads whipped to the door like guilty teenagers busted by the parents. "Oh, shit," she said and stuffed her legs through her jeans and pushed her head through her shirt.

Damn it. The show was cut short.

"There's a twenty in my pants pocket," he said. "Do you mind getting the door?"

Kiko smiled and buttoned her jeans. She knelt between his knees to dig in his pockets for the bill, and he considered skipping the pizza for round two. He'd officially lost his mind for her.

"I got it," she said with a wave of the twenty. The doorbell rang again, and while Kiko collected the pizza, Kiyoshi shuffled to the bathroom, holding himself, so he didn't make a mess. With lightning speed, he cleaned up and returned to the living room wearing only dress pants.

Kiko had carried the food to the coffee table and lifted the lid. The heavenly scent of deep-dish pizza and breadsticks drifted through his living room. Having a girl stay more than an hour in his house was a special occasion, so he'd splurged on breadsticks.

Kiyoshi returned to her side, and they dug in. He noticed her checking out his bare chest. He flexed his abs while they ate and after he swallowed, he asked, "Want me to play the movie?" It was less than half over, and he wanted an excuse for her to stay longer.

"Sure."

Biting back a grin of excitement, Kiyoshi pressed play, but no matter how much fun the movie was, the amazing woman sitting next to him captured his full attention. His eyes refused to leave her, and he was intoxicated by her scent, a tropical fragrance mixed with a throb-inducing sweat.

After they finished their food, Kiko stood.

Kiyoshi scrambled to pause the movie. "Everything okay?"

"I'll be right back." She went into the bathroom for a few minutes and came back out without her pants. Her full attention was on him with a need in her eyes even Kiyoshi wasn't blind to see. He turned the movie off.

"Show me your bedroom," she said with a tease.

Kiyoshi wanted to slap himself in the face. This couldn't be reality, and she couldn't be real. Without hesitation, he swung her up over his shoulder to a yelp and laughter. Kiyoshi brought her exactly where she asked. His house might've been in less-than-ideal conditions, but just in case this dream ever came true, he had a king-sized bed with high thread count sheets.

"Nice bed," Kiko said, noticing his second and only other splurge. "I hope we don't ruin it."

Kiyoshi groaned. "This would be the only instance where I wouldn't be upset. Don't hold back on me."

Kiko didn't, and the bed survived.

He had only known her for a few hours, but one thing was certain: He would marry her even if it killed him.

Chapter 6

KIKO'S SMILE WOULDN'T GO away the next morning as she dressed properly. Kiyoshi was still asleep in the rumpled bed. She'd set out to have a night of fun, and she exceeded her own expectations. Although she hadn't planned to spend the night. Yoshi was sexy, talented in all the important areas, and passionate about the culture he missed. There was one problem. She didn't have time for more, and Kiyoshi was the type of man to need more.

"You're up early," Kiyoshi said, leaning against the door frame with a towel around his waist. He was very nice to look at. Lean and smooth with firm curves. Kiko remembered the feel and taste of him.

"I have to go."

"How about a late breakfast? It's what?" Kiyoshi squinted at a clock on the VHS player. "Ten? I'm sure we can find biscuits and eggs somewhere. There's this great diner downtown—"

"I can't," Kiko interrupted. She promised herself only one night of fun, and she had a meeting with the real estate agent. She couldn't miss her chance at freedom.

Kiyoshi approached and reached out to touch her arms, but Kiko ducked his touch, and suddenly she struggled to meet his gaze.

He added, "How about tonight? Dinner's on me."

Kiko shook her head, regretting the answer she had to give him. She needed to focus on school. "Sorry."

With a glance at the damage she'd done, the clear heartbreak was written plainly on his face, Kiko rushed out the door. She waited at the bus stop, and she swore the curtains shifted as he watched her. The wonderful night they'd shared was tainted because she hurt him. Deep down, in the areas of her being she refused to acknowledge, she wanted to see him again. Why wouldn't she? He was amazing, but she couldn't string him along.

The bus dropped her off near home, and Kiko climbed the steps to her parents' house. Inside, the dark television screen told her Dad was gone. Mom busied herself in the kitchen doing god-knew-what. "Hey, honey," Mom said.

Kiko didn't hide that she stayed out all night. She was an adult.

"Hi, Mom." Kiko returned her mom's greeting and hauled her rear straight upstairs. In her bedroom, Kiko inhaled a fistful of her shirt's neckline. The heady scent shook her body with the memory of Yoshi's hands. She didn't want to wash him away; then the single dreamlike night would be officially over, but hygiene and reality prevailed.

Kiko pulled professional-looking clothes out of her closet and stepped into the bathroom. She cranked the hot water knob and stripped down. She retraced his caressing sensual touch, and she spent extra time washing. The mirror fogged over before she finished, and the only way to improve the shower was if Yoshi's own hands had participated.

Relaxed and ready to meet with Mr. Takai from the newspaper ad, Kiko went downstairs and unwrapped a Pop-Tart. She dropped it into the toaster.

Behind her, Mom mixed something lumpy. "Where are you going dressed like that?"

"I have a meeting."

"I see," she said, dismissively. No point in lying. Mom didn't care much about what Kiko did as long as she finished college.

Ever since she'd seen Yoshi's sword, she'd been curious about her own family's katana. Kiko asked, "Do you remember that sword Dad mentioned a few times? The one with the ratty black grip and curved markings?"

"Your great-grandfather Jiro's katana?" Mom turned to face her.

"That's the one. What happened to it?" The pastries popped out of the toaster and Kiko caught them.

"Strange of you to ask." Mom raised a brow.

Kiko had only seen a photo of it once, and Dad mentioned it only a couple times. Since any discussion about the story seemed to pull him into despair, she'd never prodded for information. But if she could get her family's sword then she could show Yoshi. On second thought, Kiko shouldn't have asked. She couldn't see Yoshi again anyway. "You know what? Never mind."

The front door opened and closed. A shuffling sound echoed from the entryway. Dad was home. Kiko braced herself for a fight.

"Perhaps you should ask him," Mom said, indicating Dad with a toss of her head.

"Ask him what?" Dad cut in, stopping at the coat rack and removing his hat.

"Kiko wants to know the katana story."

Dad's brows lifted in surprise. "Another school essay?"

Thanks for the cover, Dad. "Yeah."

"Sit on the couch, and I'll be there in a minute."

Kiko obeyed and waited for Dad to finish getting settled from whatever thing he did on Saturdays. She always thought it was poker, but she declined to question him and get reprimanded. Her dad was private, even with his own family.

Her fingers strummed against her thigh, not with impatience but anxiety. She would never rush her father. He was a stubborn and prideful man. That was where most of the fights stemmed from. Mom and Dad's stubbornness and their viewpoints on many hot topics clashed. Kiko often wondered how they'd ended up together, and even more how they stayed together.

After fifteen rather uncomfortable minutes waiting, Dad finally sat in his recliner and flipped on the television. He didn't acknowledge her presence at all. Was her request a waste of his time? Perspiration beaded on her forehead. Going to the dentist was more fun than having a chat with Dad, but she wanted the story. She cleared her throat in request, and Dad started talking.

"It was a legendary sword, made by my grandfather's grandfather, Kaneyoshi Hada, a samurai who never saw war. With decades of peace, fellow soldiers moved on to higher pursuits. Your great, great"—he counted on his fingers—"great-grandfather refused to give up tradition, insisting a threat was around the corner. In his free time, he used a technique of tempering steel and produced a fine blade with an edge that can split a fly in half.

"It had never spilled blood by the time of his death in 1806. It passed from father to son over the decades until your great-grandfather, Jiro, was next of kin. By then it was a treasured family heirloom. His little brother, Taro, fought to own it, seeing birth order as an injustice. Taro knew he couldn't beat his stronger, older brother, so rather than fight to his demise, he offered him a deal."

Kiko was glued to every word.

"See, big brother Jiro always loved the beautiful Kana, but she only had eyes for Taro. Unfortunately, Taro wasn't interested. A real life love triangle. In that respect..." Dad paused and glanced at Mom. "Jiro believed his younger brother Taro was the luckiest man in the country, but Taro's first love had always been the sword. One day, Taro saw an opportunity where both brothers could see each other as the luckiest. Jiro could have his love, Kana, and Taro could have the sword.

"After Taro explained the situation to Kana, she readily agreed to prevent the brothers from fighting to the death and eliminating the risk to Taro's life. The offer was made, the deal accepted, and Jiro married Kana. He was thrilled, but it was plain to see she lived in misery. After a few short months, the guilt wracked Jiro, but he still had his pride. He couldn't give up the woman without his brother winning both the sword and Kana. Your great-grandfather, Jiro, offered to trade the woman for the sword, after discussing it with her, of course. She enthusiastically agreed, and Kana happily married his little brother Taro. They made a big family and lived happily ever after, as the tale goes. But Taro refused to return the sword to Jiro. And the brothers never spoke again."

"Wow," Kiko said. "I had no idea."

"No, you wouldn't. The story is passed down to the firstborn, generation after generation, with the passing of the sword. I can give you the story, but I don't have the sword. Jiro eventually married and had children of his own, but the sword is rightfully yours, Kiko, but unfortunately, it had been destroyed by Jiro's angry son, who hated that the sword broke the Hada family apart, making the brothers and their descendants hate each other. The dispute lasted for generations, and since we'd all spread out over the years, most of us no longer speak." Dad scoffed. "Most of us don't even know each other."

Dad handed her a grainy photograph of a sword. It was too small and grainy to see the markings. Although Kiko couldn't impress Yoshi with her family's sword, maybe he'd still think the photograph was interesting. "Can I hold onto this for a little while?"

"Go ahead. It's the closest you'll get to owning it."

Kiko tucked the photo away and thanked her father for his time. She had her lunchtime meeting with Mr. Takai to attend, and she was beyond excited.

Chapter 7

CLICKS OF LIGHTWEIGHT BAMBOO echoed throughout the dojo hall, which wasn't much different from a gym. Along the back wall were bathrooms, locker rooms, and *Sensei*'s office. The surrounding walls were frosted glass for bright but diffuse light, and the floors were smooth hardwood for grip. The stretch of space smelled like sweat and maple. Students were expected to supply their own equipment and uniforms, but *Sensei* offered spares for those who didn't have the funds. He wanted people of all backgrounds to learn the art of kendo, and stacked neatly against one wall was a small selection of sparring weapons—*bokken* and *shinais*, face shields—*men*, bracers—*kote*, and a couple surplus *kendogis* were folded neatly. No one was ever shamed for needing it, whether they couldn't afford their own, or they forgot theirs, or they couldn't get to the laundromat on time. That was why Kiyoshi loved this dojo.

Wondering about Roger's potential against Eric Woodson the other day had Kiyoshi asking to spar. Surprisingly, Roger humored him but promised to take it easy. Kiyoshi didn't want easy. The perfect woman slipped through his fingers, and the rejection still stung. It couldn't have been his shitty house—she hadn't run when she saw it. It couldn't have been his sword—she gushed about its potential history. The problem lied somewhere with Kiyoshi himself, but he didn't know what he did or said wrong, or if it was something he could fix at all.

Roger's *shinai*, a light-colored bamboo sword with leather fittings and a sharp bite, stabbed Kiyoshi in his breastplate, his *do*. Kiyoshi's bare feet gripped the lacquered wood floors, stopping him from losing balance. The two friends circled one another while the rest of the class sparred in their own pairs. Navy blue sweeping robes of the *kendogis* spun like dancers, and Kiyoshi's mind flashed to Kiko spinning him over in bed.

Roger swung at Kiyoshi, but he parried at the last second, locked hilt to hilt, but Roger's strength was incredible. Kiyoshi gritted his teeth in effort to push the hulking man back.

On top of his weight class, Roger didn't rely on his size to win. The skill was there, as Kiyoshi expected, having watched him spar numerous times. And now Kiyoshi was going to lose from severe sleep deprivation. His mind couldn't focus on the match. Images of his long night with Kiko—her hands on him in the shower and her gyrating under his mouth—which he wouldn't trade for the world, twisted his belly.

Kiyoshi wasn't rich. He didn't own a car, couldn't afford fine dining, and he didn't have cable, but he never pretended to be something he wasn't. She slept with him and dropped him like a hot potato. Kiko used him. He'd never been used before.

Kiyoshi took a hit to the shoulder.

"What's eating you?" Roger asked. "I don't mean to puff you up, but your performance is usually more challenging."

"I was used." Kiyoshi's *men* obscured his shock. All he wanted was a girlfriend, not a one-night stand.

At Roger's puzzled face, Kiyoshi counter struck and earned a point against Roger's *kote*.

Roger shook his hand with the muted sting. "I was distracted, which is the only reason you got a point on me, man. But seriously, who used you? Do I have to break some fingers?"

Kiyoshi chuckled. "There will be no finger breaking. A girl spent the night."

"So?" Roger shifted his feet to strike.

"*With me,*" Kiyoshi clarified for his dense friend. Kiko had dressed quietly. She'd been polite and soft-spoken—nothing like the woman in the sheets the night before—and she'd refused eye contact. Was she ashamed of herself? Of him? He hoped not. Kiyoshi then offered to take her out for lunch, but she declined. In reality, he needed the commission from his lunchtime appointment. The lady was his first confirmed showing in over a week, and no commissions had panned out in three, but he would've rescheduled for one more day with Kiko. But she wanted nothing to do with him, and he needed to get her out of his mind, somehow.

Roger struck Kiyoshi on the top of his *men*, earning another point. Good. Maybe the hit would knock some sense into his thick skull. Despite knowing he was rejected, he didn't want Roger to tease. Kiyoshi'd suffered enough embarrassment already, so he explained only the highlights. "Kiko, an angel straight from my dreams, spent the whole night with me. The things she did I had only seen on tape."

"Ohhhh," Roger said, the light finally flicking to life inside his big head. "That makes sense. So, she didn't run away when she saw your place, huh?"

Kiyoshi jabbed his *shinai* and missed. "Not at all." Just the morning after. Brushing that thought aside, he added, "She was great though. A perfect fox, and I can't get my mind off her."

"Are you seeing her again?" Roger pushed forward into a consecutive attack on Kiyoshi's *kote* and *men*.

Kiyoshi swept Roger's *shinai* away, and the larger man spun into a counter strike Kiyoshi ducked. "I hope so." It was the truth, but unless she made contact, he was going to leave her alone. He respected her decision.

"Hope so? If she's wishy washy, give her my number. I'll take her for a test drive she'll never forget."

Kiyoshi lowered his *shinai*. Jealousy coursed through him. Roger had no shortage of ladies, and even though Kiko had rejected him, Kiyoshi couldn't imagine Roger seducing her. Roger wasn't as kind or respectful as she deserved. "Absolutely not," he said, and ignored the next point taken against his *do*. "You stay away from her. I mean it, Rodg. She deserves better."

"I only want to give her a ride." Through his *kendogi*, Roger made hand gestures of a woman undulating in front of him.

Kiyoshi's mind turned darkening shades of red. He ripped off his *kote*, and, forgetting all his training, he dove at Roger's *men* and gripped it in his fingers. "Kiko's not a piece of meat. What about Jessica?"

Roger freed his mask from his face and flung his *kote* aside, meeting the challenge. Kiyoshi closed the distance and his fists connected to eyes and jaws. Grunts escaped thin lips. Kiyoshi leg-swept Roger, and the big man went down. Kiyoshi climbed on his chest and swung relentlessly.

Roger yelled out a peace offering, "Hey! Stop! Yoshi, it was just a harmless comment. Back off, man." Roger's thick arms shoved Kiyoshi over.

Sensei marched up to them and barked orders to control themselves. Kiyoshi climbed to his feet and helped Roger up. They both panted like marathon runners at the end of their ropes. *Sensei* grunted his frustration, paced a few steps, and scolded them like they were insolent children. Kiyoshi ignored the lecture, trying to regain control of his anger. What was wrong with him? Roger was known for being well-traveled in bed. Why would Kiyoshi care about Roger's conquests? Kiko rejected Kiyoshi, so he had no claim to her.

The friends bowed in dismissal, and headed to the locker room.

"Dude, you need to chill," Roger said. "I say shit like that about women all the time. You know that."

"Yeah, but never about any woman I've been with." Kiyoshi closed his eyes after realizing the opening he left for a zinger, and his anger melted into irritation.

Roger grinned. "That's because you've never been with one."

Kiyoshi sighed. "None that I told you about. I'm not a virgin there, playboy."

"Not anymore you're not." Roger elbowed Kiyoshi in jest, but he wasn't in the mood.

Kiyoshi still wanted to beat the pulp out of his friend, but he needed to calm down, and getting away from Roger, even for a half hour, would do wonders for his temper. "I'm out of here. See you Monday," he said dryly.

The only consolation Kiyoshi had was Roger didn't know who Kiko was or where to find her. She was safe from his seductive, heartbreaking ways.

When she'd left his house, *Indiana Jones and the Temple of Doom* was still in his VHS player. He'd be a courteous gentleman and return it for her, even rewinding first to save a buck. Maybe Blockbuster would give up her phone number. Then he could apologize for whatever he did wrong and wish her well. After his noon appointment.

Because rent needed to be paid.

Chapter 8

THE BUS DROPPED KIKO off at the towering office building downtown. Craning her neck up at the glass facade, her mouth turned to cotton. Mr. Takai with the sexy voice had directed her to the fourth floor. It was only four. She could do this. She had to. Kiko wasn't afraid of heights, but this fancy building was definitely intimidating. The people inside these walls weren't the type to appreciate a client who needed the cheapest place available, and being a single young woman was already opening herself up to judgment. She'd figured she needed to dress the part if she wanted to be taken seriously, so black pantyhose, woven leather shoes, and a cream sweater dress fit the bill. The men probably wore suits that cost more than her monthly earnings at the Gap.

She belonged with people like Yoshi—scraping by and unashamed. She smiled to herself remembering his experience in bed, and his subsequent sweet requests for a real date. Kiko wanted to, but she just couldn't, and dwelling on things that couldn't be only made her late for something real, something that would change her life for the better. Either she swallowed her discomfort at the luxury offices before her and braced herself for judgment, or she returned to her parents' house with her tail between her legs, attempting to study through wall-shaking fights. Squaring her shoulders, Kiko pushed through the front doors.

A soft elderly woman sat behind an enormous desk. Fancy palm trees—she couldn't tell if they were real or not, but she guessed real—and shiny tile and warm brown paneling just reeked of the luxury she'd expected. Kiko swallowed a lump in her throat and stepped forward.

"Can I help you, miss?" A cigarette bounced between the woman's smiling lips. That was some serious coordination.

"I have a noon appointment with Mr. Kiyoshi Takai of Main Street Realty."

"Sure, hon, have a seat over there, and he'll be right down."

Nerves shimmied along her body, and Kiko took an empty seat next to the elevator doors. A coffee table sat in front of her, buried in magazines.

The secretary spoke plainly as if through an intercom, and her tone was almost teasing. "*Mr.* Takai, your noon is here."

Kiko fished through a massive pile of *People* magazines spread out before her. An edition of 'The Sexiest Man Alive' caught her eye, featuring Harry Hamlin from—she checked the date on the cover—last March. Kiko smiled. Probably leftovers from the secretary's personal subscription. She turned the pages, mindlessly absorbing advertisements for makeup and articles about seducing a man.

The elevator door dinged, and footsteps clattered on the fancy floor, stopping in front of her. "Ms. Hada?"

Kiko craned her neck, and her mind blanked, unable to reconcile what her eyes showed her. The magazine fell on the floor. Before her were black dress pants, a fully buttoned and pressed shirt, and gelled hair that she'd gripped between her fingers. The only thing missing on his face was a smile. Kiko picked up the magazine, dropped it on the table, and stood. "Yoshi?"

The man's eyes widened with surprise, and he stared, not responding. Either her wish to see Yoshi again created a hallucination on this man's face, or he was just as shocked as her.

Kiko's palms were sweating, and she rubbed them against her dress. "Is that really you?"

The man cleared his throat. "Kiyoshi Takai, at your service, but my friends call me Yoshi." Yoshi bowed and straightened, professional and respectful.

"Kiko Hada," she said formally, with a slight grin of amusement.

Yoshi leaned in close, and remembering the feel of his skin beneath her fingers, Kiko wanted to trail kisses from his throat all the way down. Her heart pounded in her chest as his scent filled her nose—clean soap and fresh cotton. Yoshi whispered, "If you'd prefer another agent to assist you, I can find a trusted associate."

Kiko frowned. "Why would I want someone else?"

Yoshi rubbed the nape of his neck and shifted his weight. "I thought, you know, after that morning, you didn't want to see me again. I'm not offended, but I understand if there's an awkwardness here you'd like to avoid."

Kiko needed a place as soon as possible. She could easily take Yoshi's referral, but did she want to? Warmth flooded her body, and all she could think about was touching him again. She didn't have time for a relationship, but since Yoshi was helping her find her own place so she could finish school, she didn't see the harm in spending time with him. "Your ad said, 'Find your inner peace with me'. Is that accurate?"

Yoshi smiled. "There's no false advertising here. What you see is what you get."

Kiko liked what she saw. "Let's get this started."

Yoshi beamed and gestured toward the elevators. "Come upstairs, and I'll find you just what you're looking for."

Other men in suits were already on the elevator when Kiko and Yoshi stepped inside. With space constraints, her shoulders touched his, and she sucked in a breath. Kiko's body lit up, remembering Yoshi's flexible hips and tireless mouth. And now here he was. Guilt at running away stabbed at her chest. She wanted to explain why she declined his date requests. It wasn't personal. But between school and work, juggling a boyfriend was beyond her limits right now. Perhaps if she found her own quiet place, she could study efficiently and have plenty of time left over for other...more fun things...in her life. But with the rental market right now, she didn't want to get her hopes up.

The doors dinged open, and she followed Yoshi down rows of pine desks with orange accents. As he took a seat, he gestured for her to sit across from his desk. Her heart fluttered as she faced him, and Kiko rested her purse in her lap so she had something to fidget with.

Yoshi pushed a heavy tome of genealogy off to the side of his desk. How long had he been searching for his birth parents? Kiko couldn't imagine not knowing her family's history, where she belonged, where she came from. Because of it, she knew herself and what she wanted. Yoshi must've felt lost, and her heart broke for him.

Yoshi threaded his fingers together on top of his desk. "I've got 'quiet' and 'cheap'. Any other requests to narrow down the pool?"

"Running water."

Yoshi's lips quirked up in a smile. "So, no backwoods tent. Got it. Anything else?"

Kiko couldn't think of anything else, really. She wasn't picky. She'd thought Yoshi's house—despite being clearly less than ideal—was perfect. "Something small. I don't need a lot of space."

"I think I can work with that." Yoshi's fingers tapped away on the keyboard, eyes intent on the screen. "I have a couple that meet your criteria. I'll get this printed, and we'll be on our way." Yoshi retrieved the printout from the noisy printer along the back wall and brought it over. He ripped off the side perforations and tossed the strips into a recycle bin under his desk. "Ready?" He stood over her, hand out in offer.

Her heart thumped at the prospect of touching his skin. Slowly, she took his hand and a jolt of nerves lit her up from her ears to her thighs. Kiko closed her eyes briefly and when she flung her purse over her shoulder, she smacked someone.

She turned to find a dashing blond behemoth in a fine pressed suit. She said, "Oh, I'm sorry. There's not much space here."

Yoshi stiffened, and his carefree features slid away.

"Well, hello there, babe," the broad-shouldered blond said.

Chapter 9

Babe? Seriously? Kiko frowned at Yoshi's colleague, not surprised but still annoyed at the forward pet name. The stranger radiated wealth, confidence, and a bold friendliness. Although he wasn't her type, she admired good genetics when she saw them, but she didn't need to be a psychology major to recognize an inflated ego when she heard it. Maybe it was justified, but Kiko didn't care.

Yoshi tugged at his necktie. This man, the complete opposite of Yoshi, made him very uncomfortable. Kiko wasn't sure why, but that was enough information to steer clear of him.

"What brings you out of the commercial offices to the dregs of residential, Roger?" Yoshi asked.

Kiko sensed hostility toying at the edge of his voice.

"Aren't you going to introduce me?" Roger said with a smooth voice and a crook of his lips.

"Roger Meyer, this is my client. Uh—" Yoshi broke off. Either he forgot her name or he didn't want to tell Roger what it was. Kiko didn't need to guess which was the right assumption.

"Hi, client." Roger grasped Kiko's hand and kissed her knuckles. She didn't want him touching her, but she allowed it. She didn't want Yoshi to be judged or reprimanded for an outburst on respecting bodily autonomy, which she bit back with a clench of her teeth. "Is there something else I can call you? 'Client' sounds so formal." Roger chuckled.

Kiko tipped up her chin, unwilling to show weakness in the face of a wolf. "My name is Kiko Hada."

Roger's eyes darted to Yoshi, and he grinned broadly. That was the knowing expression of a recognized name from a story told. Suddenly her respect for Yoshi teetered on a cliff. She wasn't a girl who appreciated kiss-and-tell stories, especially embellished ones. She wanted to slap Yoshi, the bastard.

"Well, anyone as hot as you deserves royal treatment. Care to join me for drinks tonight? On me." Roger winked at her.

Kiko's skin crawled. "I'm not old enough."

Roger's smile fell, and he finally released her hand. "You're not old enough to drink, but you're buying real estate?" Roger squinted at Yoshi in disapproval.

Kiko's blood pressure rose with their silent conversation. She wanted to scream at both of them. "I'm not of drinking age, and I'm not buying. Get lost." Kiko's sharp tone raised both the men's brows. Yoshi smiled, and Roger's mouth dropped open. She wasn't a little girl, so she wouldn't allow them to treat her like one.

Roger dropped the playful attitude and attempted something more sincere. "I understand. My apologies. The offer still stands if you change your mind." He leaned into Yoshi's ear and whispered, but Kiko still heard him. "I like the feisty ones. They're the best and loudest in bed."

Yoshi whispered back with a warning tone, "You forgot about Jessica already? That's a new record."

Roger shrugged.

If he was within arm's reach and all of them weren't surrounded by professionals, Kiko would've slapped Roger. For now, Yoshi shooting daggers at him with his eyes would have to suffice.

Roger patted Yoshi on the shoulder, and he shrugged it off. The blond headed back to wherever he came from, but the anger still festered as he retreated. She'd suspected this kind of treatment when she'd seen the building, but part of her hoped it wouldn't happen.

"Are you ready to go?" Yoshi asked.

She darted one last glance at the blond, who closed himself inside an office nearby, and said, "Absolutely."

Yoshi offered his hand. She wouldn't take it. Anger at Roger simmered beneath the surface, but she was still pissed at Yoshi. If the alternative real estate agent wasn't who she feared—Roger Meyer—she'd take him up on switching. Yoshi dropped his hand, features dragging down with regret.

Kiko shouldered her purse firmly and headed toward the elevator. Yoshi stayed on her heels, and he pressed the button to go down. She had much to say, but she didn't want to make more of a scene. The elevator opened, and they stepped inside, and this time, they were alone. Yoshi pressed the button for the basement. When the doors closed, he said, "I'm sorry for how he treated you. He's a good guy, just a prick with women."

As much as Roger was an ass, she wasn't mad at him right now. She folded her arms across her chest.

"I didn't want you to meet him," he said to her silence.

Kiko faced men like Roger on the regular at school. That wasn't the problem at all. Kiko faced Yoshi. "You told him about us."

Yoshi's shoulders slumped, and he rubbed the nape of his neck. "Are you ashamed? I mean, I get it. I don't compare to Roger, but if I can close a few deals, maybe the guys upstairs will notice, and someday—"

He was on the wrong track. Kiko interrupted, "I'm glad you're not like him, but you told him details. I saw it in his eyes."

Yoshi dropped his arm in defeat. "I'm sorry. He's the kind of guy you have to be careful about what you say, and I wasn't careful enough. I should've known, and I'm sorry."

"So why did you?" Kiko asked sharply.

"I didn't think I'd ever see you again," Yoshi said softly.

"So that makes telling sex stories to your asshole friends okay?"

Yoshi cringed and shifted his weight. "I deserve that."

The elevator opened to the underground parking garage. Kiko walked out ahead of Yoshi, but she didn't know where to go. Rows of dark cars were parked under fluorescent lights. Not one of them was distinguishable from another. Not only did this agency have a type with clothing, but also cars. Aside from Yoshi, she suspected most if not all of those men upstairs were carbon copies of Roger. Yoshi wasn't like them, but she wasn't ready to forgive him yet. "What kind of details did you give him?"

"I only told him you spent the night, and that you were perfect. I also mentioned not being able to get my mind off you." Yoshi gave her an apologetic lift of his lips.

Kiko cast him a side-eye.

"That was it," he added. "Roger inferred the rest."

"That's the truth?"

"Every word."

Kiko's parents fought all the time. She'd always believed if they discussed their issues as they appeared, instead of letting them fester, they could resolve the problems without the fights and growing resentment. Kiko didn't want to move through life having relationships built on grudges and unspoken anger. Yoshi was honest with her. The regret and shame was all over his beautiful face and posture. Unless she wanted another Roger to help her find a place to live, she had to fix this problem between her and Yoshi. Professional relationship or not, the air needed to be cleared. As she studied him and processed his words, she believed Yoshi. He was sweet and sincere.

He was nothing like Roger.

He was absolutely nothing like her secretive and defensive father.

Kiko's anger diffused. He bared the truth to her; it was only fair for her to give him the same, starting by keeping Yoshi as her agent. Kiko gestured toward the company cars. "Which one is yours?"

Yoshi beamed.

Chapter 10

Yoshi pulled the car into the parking lot of the first property on the list, a three-story apartment complex close to downtown. It was plain brick with basic windows and no patio doors or balconies. Kiko tried not to reject the place outright. She could only imagine how much noise the building generated, but she had to keep an open mind with her budget.

"As you can see, it's convenient for your school, and it fits your size and price criteria. Ready to see the inside?"

Kiko nodded, and they climbed out of the car. Yoshi dug in his pocket for a special key and unlocked the exterior door. Down a torn carpeted hallway that smelled like cigarette smoke, Yoshi led her up three flights of stairs, where the smoke became denser.

"Apartment 3C is right here." Yoshi unlocked the apartment door and turned on the light.

It was outdated and smelled like smoke in here too, but it was clean, small, and warm, just as she asked for. Kiko checked the bathroom for functionality and cleanliness. Loud bangs and shouts came from the unit next door, and Kiko had to wonder if the walls weren't paper. This wasn't going to work. Trying to study over that noise wasn't much different than her parents' fights, and at least her parents didn't charge rent. "Next, please," Kiko said.

"Already? Are you sure? This is a nice place and very affordable."

Having Yoshi question whether she wanted to live somewhere annoyed her. Kiko pointed to the wall. "I need quiet, and that doesn't cut it. I thought I made myself clear."

A loud bang repeated followed by a string of swears likely aimed at a television screen. Kiko recognized the anger of sports fans anywhere—her dad was the biggest. She folded her arms across her chest and popped a brow.

Yoshi cringed. "Well, it is an apartment. A certain level of noise is expected."

"Unless you're paying the rent and soundproofing the walls, I'll pass."

"Come on, I'll take you to the next place." He ran his hand through his hair, and he looked at the mess of gel left on his palm. He wiped his hand clean on his pants, and Kiko hid her laugh. He wasn't embarrassed at making a mess of himself in front of her, and she couldn't help but find it endearing. Even though he'd apologized up and down, he'd violated her trust.

KIYOSHI HAD WISHED TO see Kiko again—the woman dedicated to her studies to help people struggling in their relationships, the woman who showed sincere interest in the tiny piece of his family history. That night, before and after they'd had sex all over his house, Kiko was perfect—bold, assertive, and free spirited. Exactly who he'd always dreamed of finding, the woman he wanted to scoop up forever. But that dreamlike woman didn't exist. The next morning she'd been soft spoken and shy, and now this Kiko was distant and calculating. He didn't know what to think of her many sides.

What happened to that girl? And which one was the real one? Maybe she was just pissed off, and she had a right to be. He made a stupid move, and he hurt her. He'd learned his lesson about Roger the hard way, and he wouldn't make that mistake again.

Kiyoshi drove her to the next location on his short list, eager to have this over with and a pittance of a commission in his pocket. After their fight in the parking garage, she hadn't spoken a word to him except short snippets rebuffing everything he pointed out about the properties. "Are you okay?"

"I'm fine." Her arms were crossed over her chest. He was certain she wasn't fine.

"Are you still mad at me?"

"No."

Was that a relief? Kiyoshi wasn't sure. But there was something going on. She just wasn't ready to talk about it. He'd lost all enthusiasm for his client. Trying to keep the energetic salesman pitch going was impossible. Maybe sales wasn't for him. The sooner she picked a place, the sooner this awkwardness would be over, and he wouldn't have to see her again.

Kiyoshi parked the car at the curb. "This next one here is a duplex. It's farther out of the city, but it checks all your other boxes."

Without a word or a hint of her feelings on this one, Kiyoshi led Kiko up to the porch, and he unlocked one of the twin front doors. He climbed the narrow set of stairs to the second floor, and Kiko followed behind. The musty carpet smelled of stale beer, but he'd seen and smelled worse.

Kiyoshi opened the door at the top of the stairs and stepped inside. The kitchen was a small prefab cabinet unit—not inviting, but functional. The living room had orange shag carpet, which on its own felt great on the toes, but combined with the smell, he cringed at what lurked beneath.

While he waited in the living room, Kiko assessed the placed top to bottom. Despite his better judgment, he checked her out every time she turned her attention. He couldn't help himself. She was stunningly beautiful, and he'd seen the smooth skin under those clothes. That dress of hers was sexy as hell, and he wanted to slide his hands up her thighs.

Kiko went into the bathroom and flicked on the light.

Kiyoshi adjusted himself. He might've written off Kiko in his mind, but he could still remember all the things she did, and that was a memory he'd treasure. A memory he'd compare all his future girlfriends against. Whether that was fair or not, it was the truth. "What do you think?" he called over.

"This one is a pass," she said and returned to him. "For the price, I'd just stay at my parents house. Is that vomit over there?" She pointed to a lump on the carpet.

"I don't know." Because he didn't, but also he didn't want to fight her on the place. He wouldn't want to live somewhere he hated too. The sooner he brought her to the last property, the sooner this was over. Whether or not she picked a place, he was done. "Let's go."

Kiko nodded and when they climbed into the car, he hesitated to start the engine. Kiyoshi couldn't help this electric feeling in his body being so near her. He wanted to touch her so badly. His eyes drifted over to her palms resting on her thighs. He had his face right there, but like all the closed doors today, that one was shut and locked.

"Something wrong?" she asked.

Kiyoshi drummed the steering wheel. "I can't do this."

"Do what?"

"I can't sit here and pretend things are okay between us. Clearly you hate me, and I get it. I deserve it, so to end your discomfort, I'm dropping you as a client. I'll bring you back to the office, and I'll refer you to someone else. I don't think they'll find anything different than I have, but I can't keep this up. This was a mistake." Kiyoshi stared out the windshield, unable to meet her gaze, and with nothing but silence on her end, Kiyoshi started the car.

Kiko's hand gripped his forearm. "Wait."

Kiyoshi shifted into park and waited.

"You're right."

Kiyoshi faced her. She gave him a sad smile.

"You apologized, and I accepted it, but I still treated you awful today. That wasn't fair to you, and I'm sorry. I don't want a different agent, Yoshi. I want you, but if you still want to drop me, I understand. We don't all deserve second chances."

A spark of hope ignited his chest. "Then who is the real Kiko?"

The beautiful woman next to him checked her watch and grinned. "You have one more hour to figure it out."

A sheet of cosmic water drowned out the tiny spark, and disappointment squeezed his chest. Kiyoshi started the car and drove them toward the last address. Kiko faced the side window, blocking his view of her features. He should've put his foot down—taken a page from the Kiko handbook of standing her ground. He should've brought her to the agency and wished her well. But he wanted to be the nice guy, and she did apologize, so he needed to get over his personal issues with her. Clearly, she was over him.

Not soon enough, Kiyoshi brought her to the single-family home with two bedrooms and one bathroom. It even had a private driveway, not that she had a car. It was near a bus stop and recently updated. It would be perfect for her. He pulled into the driveway and killed the engine.

"This place looks great," she said, craning her neck to see it. "What's the catch—cockroaches?"

He chuckled. "I guess we'll see when we get in there."

He unlocked the front door, and having fallen into a pattern, Kiko followed him inside. He double-checked the address with bewilderment. This place was great.

"Wow," Kiko said, spinning around. The living room had new hardwood floors. The walls were freshly painted.

And there were enough cabinets to make a U-shaped kitchen. The dishwasher and refrigerator appeared new. Kiko disappeared on her inspection, more excited than he'd seen her since *Indiana Jones and the Temple of Doom* became the soundtrack to their couch festivities.

"It has laundry right here," she called from around the corner. "And the bathroom's nice. Come check it out."

Amused, he walked into the bathroom. She stood there, lit up under the lights like sunshine kissing her hair. He wanted to strip her down and take her into the shower with him—just like last time.

"It's great," he said, voice rough with lust.

"Yeah, it is. So, what's wrong with it?"

"You aren't naked," Kiyoshi blurted.

Kiko's head turned, and her eyes widened. She held out her hands in defense. "Look, you're great in bed, but I'm not looking to date anyone right now. I'm sorry if I led you on. That wasn't my intention."

The silence stretched while Kiyoshi considered. "If you didn't want a relationship, then what do you call what we had?"

"A one-night stand. Never had one before?"

"Ouch." He raked his hands through his gelled hair again, and immediately regretted it. "I'm not a one-night-stand kind of guy."

"I'm getting that impression." Kiko sighed. "I'm sorry for...everything."

"Don't be. That was the best night of my life." It was true, one hundred percent.

Kiko's jaw dropped in shock, and her cheeks flushed.

"Scout's honor," he added.

"For real?"

"Absolutely."

Chapter 11

At first, Kiko couldn't believe she was Yoshi's best night ever, but considering he wasn't the one-night-stand kind of guy, and he appeared to be single for a while, maybe she was right about him—he wasn't very experienced. And now Yoshi was going to remember her forever. Being someone's best time was unfair pressure. With her schooling, the reason she didn't want a relationship, Kiko couldn't handle even more pressure. She couldn't fault Yoshi for wanting a repeat of his best time, and she admired him for not wanting to give up, but she wanted to run. If she rushed to the nearest bus stop, Yoshi would catch up. She needed to get away, and the only way to do that was to finish the hunt for a rental. And this newly remodeled single family home was pretty damned great. *Close the deal, get the hell away.*

"Can we...can we finish this?" Kiko asked, stumbling with Yoshi's secret crushing her.

"Sure, of course. What do you need from me?" Fire in his eyes had Kiko stepping back.

She needed space. But to get that, Kiko asked, "There's got to be something wrong with this house to fit my list of criteria. Did someone die in here? You have to disclose that, right?"

Yoshi checked his paperwork. "No murders, crack, or ghosts reported here. The remodel was likely because it needed it, and the landlord could charge more rent. Standard stuff."

Kiko narrowed her eyes. "How much is it?"

"Four hundred, water and electric included."

Kiko would never afford that with her job at the Gap. As much as that was disappointing, at least this hunt was over and she could finally get away. Returning to her parents wasn't the worst thing she could imagine. Deflated, Kiko said, "We're done here."

"Too expensive?"

"I gave you what I could afford and you wasted my time."

"That wasn't my intention. What about roommates?" Yoshi offered. "This place is awesome. Having a little help might make it worth it."

"I can't guarantee they'll be any quieter than what I live with now." It was best she stayed home and struggled her way through the noise. At least she didn't have to worry about affording tuition on top of everything else. Kiko's stomach growled. Their noon meeting meant she'd skipped lunch and coupled with defeat, she wasn't in the mood any longer. "Let's go."

Yoshi's hand touched her arm. "There are no guarantees in life. There's just living it and making changes when things don't go to plan."

Wanting to believe his optimism, Kiko asked, "Are there any other options?"

"I can try a wider range if you're willing to commute."

Adding extra stops on her bus line wouldn't be easy, and that could jeopardize her job. Without being able to pay tuition, she was back at square one. "I'd rather avoid it."

Yoshi released her. "What you're looking for is impossible. I don't believe 'perfect' exists. Sometimes good enough is just right."

Kiko didn't want to settle, and of course a cheap quiet house existed somewhere, but maybe Yoshi had the right idea. She needed a roommate, but one she knew would be respectful of her need for quiet, one who had a large peaceful house, where the neighboring house was vacant. A few minutes ago, she wanted to run away, the pressure too much to bear, but now, maybe Yoshi might have her sanctuary. "How much is your rent?"

"My rent? Why?" Yoshi tilted his head. "I don't see how that's relevant to the price range you're looking for."

"What if, hear me out, you and I split rent? Your place fits what I'm looking for. It's big enough for both of us."

Yoshi's eyes lit up with a hungry fire of unspoken promises, the same intensity from their date night. Her toes curled at his delicious thoughts, but she batted them away.

"You want to be my roommate?" he choked out.

Kiko held out her palms. She didn't want him getting the wrong idea. "To be clear, this is a business transaction. I would get what I need, and you'd have a break on the rent. With us together, we can make the place great...as roommates."

Yoshi raked a hand through his hair and his face scrunched in disbelief—not at all the reaction Kiko expected. Ignoring the gel on his hand, he said, "I can't believe you're asking me that. Are you off your rocker? I can't get you to eat dinner with me, but you're willing to move into my house. Do you have any idea how insane that sounds?"

Kiko's hopes sunk once again. She thought for sure he would go for it, but she wasn't willing to give up just yet. "I do have friends, but most of them, and the few classmates I'm friendly with, are married, have kids, or they live with their boyfriends or parents. I can't afford on-campus housing, but since it's party central, it doesn't matter anyway. So it makes sense, doesn't it? I could help make the place feel more like home. We can take turns making dinner, and I promise not to use all the hot water." Seeing all the great possibilities, Kiko smiled.

Yoshi only glared.

Softly, Kiko said, "I don't have any other options."

"I don't want to be your last choice."

"It's not personal, Yoshi; it's mutual beneficially, but this all hinges on one condition."

Yoshi scoffed. "What else would you like to add to this crazy idea? I'm not putting sequined pillows on the couch, just so we're clear, and absolutely no fuzzy rugs or *Tiger Beat* posters. You might be picky and uptight, but I have standards too." He folded his arms across his chest. His face flickered, and he smeared his hand on his shirt.

Kiko smiled. He was agreeing to her idea without saying it plainly. "We might not know each other very well—"

"I'd say we know more than we should," he interrupted.

She deserved that. "I need you to respect my study time, and I can work around the weekend sports games on your TV. So are you a party-type guy? Because if you're looking for a reason to walk out that door and leave me hanging, here's your chance." She wasn't above using a little guilt to sway him.

Yoshi glared and answered with a calm determination. "You want a business transaction, you got it. Hundred and fifty a month, and we split the heat bills. And just so we're clear, I'm doing this because it is 'mutually beneficial'. No lease. If this isn't working out, you go. Got it?"

"Thank you," Kiko answered with a smile. "I like an honest salesman." Who treated her like an adult. He was fair, and she appreciated it. "But on that note, will you help me move in? I didn't budget for movers, and I don't have a truck."

Yoshi's posture softened, and he held out a hand to shake. "You rent a pickup. I'll bring the muscle, roommate."

"Deal." Kiko took his hand and shook forcefully, fighting the urge to jump and flail around like an excited child. She got what she wanted—a quiet, affordable rental that would allow her to focus on finishing school. Kiko ignored the fire surging through her body at his touch.

"What temperature do you like the house at night?" he asked. "Because we might as well hash that out before it's too late to back out."

Kiko laughed. Nothing could go wrong now.

Chapter 12

Kiyoshi's palms were sweaty as he pulled the company car to the curb in front of Kiko's parents' house. She lived in a great home in an old established neighborhood. Kids could play in the streets here, and people wouldn't have to lock their doors at night. "This is a nice place. It doesn't sound too loud here."

"Are you trying to talk me out of moving?"

"No, just trying to understand."

Kiko rested her fingers on the door handle. "Just because it looks nice on the outside, doesn't mean everything is smooth on the inside."

Kiyoshi inferred, "Your parents fight? Is that why you want to be a marriage counselor?"

"You got it," she said softly.

His heart broke for her. Listening to parents who yell, scream, break things, and can't function without drama was exhausting. His parents were the opposite—buttoned up, closed off, and always calm. He could never tell what was going through their minds, but the only thing he knew for sure—they didn't want him to know about his birth parents. Of course, that only drove him to know more. The sooner he could get Kiko out of there, the safer she would be.

"When do you want to do this?" he asked.

"Is tomorrow too soon?"

Not soon enough. "I think I can make that work. I'll let you know if it doesn't."

"Great." Kiko smiled and hesitated before climbing out of the car.

Kiyoshi wanted to lean in for a kiss, feeling like it was the natural thing to do. He stared at her mouth and gazed into her eyes, silently pleading for the hope so desperate to survive.

Kiko didn't shift toward him, but maybe she just needed a little sign that it was okay. Kiyoshi leaned toward her, but Kiko turned and climbed out of the car.

Too soon. He needed to be far more patient.

Kiko walked up the steps, and just before stepping inside, she glanced at Kiyoshi over her shoulder.

That had to mean something.

There was hope.

When the house swallowed her whole, Kiyoshi finally pulled away from the curb. His head spun with everything that just happened. Kiko had been upset with him for spilling details of their night together, but she accepted his apology. When he thought he had an opportunity to take her out, she rejected him. But now she offered to be his roommate. When she'd asked, he was so damned excited, but he had a shred of dignity left. He made her work for it, and now he had a sexy roommate and half the rent bill. A spear of fire ran through him. He pictured nights of exposed skin, sweat, and cries of pleasure. And the best part? It was her idea.

The sex was amazing, criminal even, but he wanted more than romps in the sheets, and now he had time to earn a real date. Kiyoshi wanted it all—the spooning, the cuddles on the couch, holding hands in public. He wanted to know her fears, her hopes, and her dreams. Hell, he'd love to help her study. Kiyoshi wanted to wake up to a beautiful woman with his rock-solid cock looking for an invitation—and getting accepted. He couldn't think of a single downside to this arrangement, and he was dumbstruck with his unusual good luck.

Living with her parents, Kiko shouldn't have too much to bring, furniture being the worst of the job. Whatever she had, he'd accept, since his house needed more than spare second-hand furnishings to feel like home, and if she wanted fluffy rugs or sequined pillows, he'd gladly display them.

Deep down, Kiyoshi was a sap.

Kiyoshi returned the company car to the underground parking garage and hitched a ride on the bus home. He pictured where her stuff would go, and he wanted to scrub his house from top to bottom so she wouldn't be surprised by hibernating dust bunnies in the closet of his spare bedroom. He climbed off the bus and lightly jogged home, loosening the tie at his throat and enjoying the exertion. Energy pumped through him as he pushed into his house and assessed the place with new eyes.

First thing's first. He needed to secure the muscle, and until he got his friends to show up, promises were just words. This had to happen. Kiyoshi crossed to the phone on the wall and dialed Eric Woodson's number. His best friend answered on the second ring, sounding groggy with sleep.

"Woodson, how's it going?"

"It's Saturday afternoon, Yoshi. Why are you up so early?"

Woodson's family owned a publishing house, and he was finishing college to join the ranks. Friday nights were always dedicated to parties, and Saturdays for sleeping in, but this couldn't wait. "I had to work today. Listen, is there any chance you can help move furniture tomorrow?"

"Yoshi, you can't leave. I need my sparring partner."

"I'm not going anywhere. I'm moving someone in."

"Oh, that's a relief. I wish I could help, but my girlfriend's got this thing tomorrow I promised. Some girly fair. Trust me, I'd much rather help you."

Damn it. Kiyoshi paced. "Don't worry about it. I'll see you at kendo."

"You bet."

Kiyoshi pressed the receiver down and waited for the dial tone. He dialed the numbers of six other friends from the dojo. Half of them were busy, and the other half didn't answer. Kiyoshi swore again. There was only one person left on his list—the last person he wanted to call, who was currently in a time out. But, Roger had the strength of two men, possibly three.

"Roger," Kiyoshi said after the third ring.

"Yoshi." Roger mirrored him. "It's Saturday. I'm not talking shop until I'm on the clock."

"This isn't about work." There had to be a way Kiyoshi could secure Roger's help without him finding out Kiko was the roommate in question, which would keep her safe from his sharp tongue. Right now, Kiyoshi wanted nothing more than for her to move in.

"Okay then. What's going on?"

"Are you free to help move furniture tomorrow?"

Roger chuckled. "Who's moving where? 'Cause I know you don't have any."

Kiyoshi hesitated, but he needed Roger's strength. "I found a roommate, and I need muscle."

"For that you called the right guy."

Clearly. "So what do you say?"

"Letting someone move in is only going to hinder your game. It's much easier to get laid when you live alone, but it's your choice. Are you prepared for your new roommie to be banging chicks right next to you?"

Roger's question was a splash of icy water on Kiyoshi's head. He'd never considered for a second that if Kiko didn't give him another chance, she could bring home dates. How would he feel listening to her sexy noises with someone else in one of his bedrooms? Devastated. Tortured. More than he could bear, but he'd told her outright if this wasn't working out, she had to leave.

Kiyoshi came up with a viable lie. "We're not all made of money Roger."

His friend, still in the doghouse, chuckled in his ear. "I told you, commercial real estate is where it's at."

"I'll consider it," Kiyoshi said, dismissively. "So, can I count on you or not?"

"Since you're broke, pay me in pizza and beer, and it's a deal."

Kiyoshi smiled and recited Kiko's parents' address. "Be there sharp and ready to lift."

"I got it. I'll be there." Roger disconnected the call.

Kiyoshi exhaled. He'd just given Kiko's address to Roger, but he didn't know it was hers. He didn't know Kiyoshi's new roommate was a woman at all. If Roger arrived when he was supposed to, her parents would be out of the house, and Kiyoshi would be there as point guard to make sure Roger behaved and Kiko didn't antagonize him. The plan couldn't fail.

Chapter 13

KIKO HAD SPENT ALL evening and late into the night sorting and organizing her room, and after her shift at the Gap Sunday morning, Kiko brought home flattened boxes. Her parents were at church as expected. She should've let them know her intentions at some point during the week, but since it wasn't a sure thing, she didn't want to give them expectations and fail to live up to them. The three of them were like ships sailing in opposite directions. Her parents didn't care when she came or went, so they wouldn't care where she closed her eyes to rest at night. All they drilled into her head was her finishing college, which was also her biggest priority.

Kiko changed out of her work polo and opened up and taped the bottoms on a stack of boxes. She didn't have much to pack—school supplies, clothes, her prized Michael J. Fox poster, a lamp, and toiletries. She also packed the awards and certificates she'd earned—science fair and academic excellence. The last thing left was a photograph of her with her parents, taken back in the day before the fighting started. Kiko was about seven years old. Her parents leaned in close with her in the middle, and all three of them smiled with real love. Kiko double checked her dresser drawers and found the grainy photograph Dad had given her of Jiro's katana. She slipped it into her back pocket.

Was it convenient or depressing that her entire life fit into a dozen boxes? Right now, convenient. Later she'd try not to think about it. Since her parents weren't home to ask, she would leave behind her bedroom furniture. She felt silly asking for muscle now. She might've handled this herself in three or four trips on the bus. Would've been cheaper than renting a pickup too, but good thing she didn't get one yet.

Kiko dragged her boxes downstairs and stacked them by the door. She wrote a quick note to her parents, giving them her new address and Yoshi's phone number. She folded the note and placed it on the kitchen counter in the shape of a little tent so they might notice it.

The doorbell rang. Yoshi hadn't told her how much muscle or what their names were, but she appreciated everyone showing up. Kiko checked the clock on the wall. They were early too. Good thing she was prepared.

Kiko rushed to the door and swung it wide. She sucked in a breath at the behemoth blocking her door. Roger Meyer was the last person she'd expected Yoshi to call for help, but Kiko asked for a big favor, and she could play nice. "Hi, Roger."

His smile radiated a million dollars, or more likely, good dental insurance and a bunch of pocket money. He was traditionally handsome and even more stunning in a striped polo and jeans. Aviator sunglasses hid his roaming eyes. He wore a short trim beard and his blond hair was teased to new heights. Kiko saw through it all. She also knew he was only friendly because of Yoshi's bedroom stories. She wasn't mad at Yoshi anymore. He'd screwed up and he apologized, but Roger was something else entirely.

She stepped back, and his head craned toward her boxes. Kiko gave herself a mental shake and remembered he was only here to help. Just like she didn't want to be judged at first glance by Main Street Realty's suits, she shouldn't judge Roger too quick either. "Thanks for helping. Come on in." She stepped aside, and his bulk took up most of the door frame.

"Nice digs, Kiko." He took off his sunglasses and hooked them onto the neckline of his shirt. He casually looked around like a first-time guest would.

"Thanks. I really appreciate the help." Kiko leaned out of the door, looking for the rest of the crew. "Where's everyone else?"

He smiled at photos hanging on the walls. "Parents aren't here?"

"Not at the moment." Roger hadn't asked about where she was moving. He hadn't asked about the truck. He made no move to lift a single box, and he was alone. Warning hairs lifted on her arms. "But I'm expecting them back any second. Did Yoshi come with you?" Hopefully Roger didn't hear the uncertainty in her voice.

Roger retraced his steps to her and closed the front door. "He'll be along shortly." His dazzling smile returned, but its charms didn't work.

Kiko shifted her weight uncomfortably. "Sure. Well, I didn't get the truck yet."

Roger approached the stack of boxes and placed his hands on his hips, assessing the workload. "Is this it?"

"That's everything." Kiko was glad to get back to business. Roger was definitely not her type, but that didn't mean he was a threat in any way. Yoshi wouldn't be friends if he was truly a bad person.

"We don't need a truck for this. I can pack these into the trunk and back seat of my coupe. It might take two trips, maybe, but this isn't a big deal." His hand waved over Kiko's things.

She smiled and assumed he'd locked his car. "That's a good plan. When should we get started?"

"Yoshi's not here yet, so, I guess we have a lot of time." Roger's slight shift in tone didn't go unnoticed.

Kiko's blood chilled, and instinctively, she inched backward toward the front door. She should've listened to the little red flags waving dramatically, but she picked them up now. When her fingers brushed against the door, she put her hand on the knob behind her. "We don't have *that* much. My parents are on their way home right now." She hoped.

Roger's eyes smoldered while he prowled closer and leaned over her. The scent of aftershave and pine needles stung her nose. The deadbolt tumbler thumped over, and Kiko exhaled a shaky breath.

The blond gestured to the couch. "Have a seat. I know you aren't twenty-one yet, but are you adventurous enough to have a beer with us?"

"Umm, I guess so."

"Great." Roger wrapped a meaty arm over her shoulders and guided her to the couch. She sat uneasily, and Roger picked Dad's recliner to sink into. He leaned forward on his elbows and steepled his fingers. "Yoshi worked hard to leave his parents' house. They were awful. Did you know that?"

They were cold and distant, but Kiko shook her head. Anything to keep him talking.

"I tried to talk him into joining my team. Commercial real estate is where the real money is, but Yoshi wanted to work with regular people. Like you. The commissions are pitiful in comparison. He skipped meals to make it happen, and I picked up the tab for him a number of times. All he wants is a girlfriend, the poor sap. I keep telling him if he has money, he can have any girl he wants."

Kiko's stomach churned. Maybe Roger wasn't that different from what she'd first thought.

"So when he told me he was getting a roommate, I had to do something. After he gave me the address, a simple property record search told me who was going to ruin his single life. I honestly didn't think it was a woman, and I certainly didn't think it was you."

"What is that supposed to mean?"

"I hear you can do amazing things, and now I understand."

Swallowing back her disgust, Kiko said, "So are you here to help or insult me?"

Roger smiled. "I'm here to help."

Whether he was a threat or not, she needed to keep him calmly under control until Yoshi got here. "Did you bring the beer?"

"Yoshi is."

Okay, another idea. "My parents have wine if you don't want to wait for a drink."

Roger stood. "Don't mind if I do."

"It's in the fridge."

Roger stalked over to the refrigerator and stuck his head inside. He retrieved the bottle and rummaged in the cabinets.

Kiko glanced at the clock. How much longer until Yoshi arrived? And where were her parents? "Glasses are above the dishwasher."

Roger poured two glasses. Not three or five or however many hands were supposed to come. Kiko twisted to look out the large picture window behind the couch, searching for Yoshi approaching from the bus stop. There was no one.

Roger held out a glass of red, and she accepted it. He sat next to her this time. Kiko only swallowed a few sips. Roger downed his whole glass and sighed with contentment.

"You know, since the second I saw you at the office, I knew you were different." Roger chuckled, and Kiko continued to nurse her drink. "I told my girlfriend about you, and she figured out in a flash that you were special. She's a quick one."

Kiko kept her eyes on the carpet, focusing on her peripheral vision.

"Want to know why?"

"Sure, Roger. Why am I different?"

"I couldn't stop talking about you, and Jessica got all jealous and dumped me. I heard you weren't interested in Yoshi, so I was thinking I should take you out to dinner tonight. Celebrate your new home."

Kiko was part flattered, and part skeeved out. "It sounds like a nice offer, Roger, but I must decline. Yoshi was right.

I have too much going on in my life, and I'm in the middle of moving. It's just not the right time for me."

"'Just not the right time' is an excuse to hide from the adventures of life. I'll show you what you're missing out on."

"I can't, really." Catching onto that warning, Kiko stood, but Roger gripped her back pocket and pulled. Red wine splashed out of her glass.

Roger rose in a panic, staring at his clothes, but they were clean. In his fingers was the photo from her back pocket. "What's this?" Roger glanced at the legendary katana. Disinterested, he dropped it onto the carpet as if it were a piece of trash. "Now where were we?"

"I was getting a refill. I think you could use one too. And now there's a mess to clean up."

Roger wrapped his meaty arms around her, and Kiko dropped the glass. "Kiss me."

"Roger, let me go."

"I won't ask twice."

Angry at Roger's disrespect, Kiko said, "And I won't tell you twice. Get your hands off me and get out of my house." Kiko struggled in his arms, but she couldn't break free.

Roger chuckled, a dark, stomach-curdling sound that would haunt her nightmares. "Time's up."

Having no other defense, Kiko did the one thing she could. She screamed bloody murder, forcing Roger to cover his ears with his hands. It worked, but he slapped her so hard it sounded like wood cracking against its frame, and white blinding pain washed over Kiko's head.

Chapter 14

Kiko's terrifying scream gutted him. Kiyoshi's legs ate up the ground in a surge of panic. At her door, he shouted her name and tried the knob, but it was locked. Kiko's second scream punched his heart. He had no time to see if someone would come to the door and let him in. Kiyoshi backed up and threw himself at the wood with a kick, but it only cracked. The deadbolt had been turned, otherwise he would've been through it. Kiyoshi raced around the house, looking for open windows, but there were none. In a stroke of luck, the back door wasn't locked, and he bolted through it.

Blood pumped in his ears, rage blinding him to everything but the enemy hurting Kiko. When he found her, he stopped short. Roger slapped Kiko across the face, and Kiyoshi went feral. He wanted to tear every limb from Roger's body in a savage attack the brute would never forget, training be damned. But knowing his strength and that of his opponent, he restrained himself.

"Get your hands off her," Kiyoshi yelled.

Roger didn't react fast enough, and Kiyoshi couldn't wait. Kiko couldn't wait.

Kiyoshi brushed a lamp off an end table and lifted it by the leg. He launched it at Roger's spine, and with a loud thwack, her assailant dropped to the floor like a sack full of bricks. Kiko's terrified face crushed him. He rushed to her side, and Kiko fell into his arms. He pressed her against him. "You're okay now. It's okay. I got you."

Her breaths pulled in with jerky motions, but she was safe. Kiyoshi always knew Roger was a pig, but he didn't know Roger was a monster. What if he were just a few minutes later? A few minutes was the difference from everyone being okay to something unthinkable.

Kiyoshi stroked her hair. "Damn it, Kiko, I'm sorry. This shouldn't have happened. He was the only one who could help, and I had my reservations, but I—I screwed up. I'm so sorry."

Kiko pulled back enough to meet his apologetic gaze. "His actions aren't your fault, but I'm glad you came. I hate to think of what he was willing to do."

Kiyoshi tucked a stray lock of her dark hair behind her ear. "I won't let him hurt you again. You have my promise."

Tears filled Kiko's eyes, and Kiyoshi pulled her back into a hug again. His hands rubbed her back in smooth circles. She felt right in his arms, and he never wanted to let her go. "But that end table was entirely my fault. I'll replace it."

"Don't worry about it." Her breathing calmed down, and Kiyoshi reluctantly released her.

Roger hadn't moved.

"Should we call an ambulance?" Kiko asked.

"More like the cops." Roger deserved to be arrested for that.

"I doubt he'd be charged. It's my word against his. Who do you think they'll believe?" Kiko asked.

Kiyoshi didn't want to answer that—a rich, well-connected white man or a Japanese-American woman from the middle-class 'burbs? "Let me check him." Kiyoshi folded down at the asshole's side and jostled his shoulder. Roger softly grunted, and his eyelids twitched. "He's alive."

"That's good enough for me," Kiko said.

A flicker of something on the carpet caught his attention. Kiyoshi reached and picked up a photograph. His heart skipped at the sight of it, yellowed with age and torn at the corners, wrinkled all over. "Where did this come from?"

Kiko took the photograph from him and slipped it into her back pocket. "Can we talk about it later? I don't want to be around when Roger wakes up."

He had a million questions, but she was right. Roger was going to be pissed when he came around, and the two of them needed to be far away until he cooled off. "Let's get out of here."

Kiko led him to the stack of boxes by the front door. "I didn't get the truck yet."

"Grab a couple, and I'll get a stack. We'll take the bus and get the rest another time."

Kiko pointed out which ones were priority since they couldn't get them all in one go. They filled their arms. The boxes were light, thankfully, and they brought them to the bus stop. Roger hadn't left the house before the bus pulled up. Hopefully he wasn't wrecking the place in retaliation. Kiyoshi waited for Kiko to board ahead of him, and the farther the bus ambled down the road, the more they both relaxed.

Once inside his house, Kiyoshi unloaded her boxes in his bedroom. He moved to the closet and shoved aside the hangers with his clothes. "I haven't had a chance to empty out the spare bedroom, so you can have this half of the closet." He rubbed the nape of his neck. "And until we can get your bed, I'll sleep on the couch. You can have mine."

"That's unnecessary. We can sleep next to each other like adults. It's not like we haven't before."

Heat flushed through Kiyoshi and tightened his pants as the memories rushed through his mind. Kiyoshi would not argue. "I have no problem with that."

While Kiko began unpacking, Kiyoshi sat on the bed. "I hope Roger calms his ass down quickly."

"Yeah, I don't need him breaking in here next," Kiko said, stuffing a hanger into a shirt.

"I need to ask him how he had a photograph of my sword that looks like it's seventy years old."

Kiko stilled. "Are you sure it's yours?"

The desperation for keys to his past made the leap in an instant. "I'd recognize those grainy marks anywhere. Why did you take it with?"

Kiko fished the photograph out of her pocket and handed it to him. She sat, their thighs touching. For the first time, his brain wasn't visualizing a repeat of their date night. She said, "It's not his."

Kiyoshi made the logical leap. "It's yours."

Kiko nodded.

Hurt swirled in his chest. "You knew about my sword this whole time, but you didn't tell me?"

"My dad told just me the story and gave me that photo. I wasn't even sure if it was yours. I was going to talk to you about it. I know how much this all means to you."

Kiyoshi's mind blanked. "What story?"

"Well, a convoluted story short—as firstborn, my great grandfather was the rightful owner, but his younger brother cheated him of it, and the sword passed down through his bloodline instead. This photo is the only remaining proof of the sword. Everyone thought it was destroyed."

Kiyoshi caught onto the implications of Kiko's confession. She knew his relatives. A link, a lead, something that showed him where he belonged. "My birth family. You know who my parents are?"

"I can find out."

"I must know, please," he begged. Then he realized the other implication of what Kiko confessed. "If you're descended from the sword's owner, and the stranger who delivered the sword to my adoptive parents was also a descendant..." Kiyoshi trailed off.

Kiko finished, "If and if, then there's a chance we're distantly related. Kaneyoshi Hada had two sons, but the family tree ballooned from there. I know all my first and second cousins, so if we're related, we aren't very close."

"He's a Hada?" Kiyoshi finally had a name.

"As the story goes." Kiko mirrored his line with a small lift of her lips. "But I think the priority here is finding out if we're related, because, well, you can imagine..."

Ick factor. "I agree."

Kiyoshi's landline phone rang. He leaned over to the bedside table and answered it. He offered it to Kiko. "It's for you."

Kiko accepted the phone, and Kiyoshi waited by her side. "Hello?"

"Hi, honey, it's Mom."

"Mom!" Kiko said in a rush. "Is everything okay?"

"I found your note. What happened to the end table?"

Kiyoshi's cheeks heated.

Kiko met his gaze. "A moving accident. I'll take care of it. I'm sorry."

She didn't need to apologize for him destroying her parents' property, but he appreciated her covering. Since her mother wasn't ranting about an unconscious body in her living room, Roger must've woken up and left. And since she wasn't flipping about more than the end table, he hadn't destroyed the house in his wake. That was a relief.

"And the wine on the floor?"

Kiko startled and exchanged a worried glance with Kiyoshi. "I'll get it cleaned up."

"Don't worry about it. Accidents happen. Are you sure moving out is best right now?" her mother asked. "School is very important, and I don't want anything to derail you."

"I need a break, Mom. I need space."

"You have your own bedroom. What more space do you need?"

Kiko pressed a palm against her forehead. "I need *quiet* to study."

Her mom stayed silent for a few beats. Kiyoshi knew what Kiko referenced.

"I see. I understand. We should've talked to you before you felt the need to do something like this." Her mother's voice was low and shameful.

"I need to be on my own. It's not personal."

Kiyoshi knew that wasn't true. Kiko didn't want to move in with him to save money or because she cared for him. This was a business transaction. She needed to escape her stressful home environment.

"Well, I've got so much furniture around here. Do you need any? You can have your bed, dresser, night stand. I've got extra kitchen chairs and a recliner downstairs. I'd love to unload on you." Her mother's tone was much brighter now, excited even, that her daughter found independence.

"Thanks. I appreciate it." Kiko's eyes watered, and she glanced at Kiyoshi again. His heart skipped a beat. "Hey, wait. Mom?"

"Yeah?"

"Can I get a copy of our family tree going all the way back to great grandfather Taro and his brother Jiro?"

"Sure, honey. I'll make a photocopy for you tomorrow and leave it in your room. Your old room."

Kiko returned the headset to the receiver with a sad smile on her face. "Tomorrow I'll have the family tree, and you'll finally have answers."

"You have no idea how much that means to me."

"I think I do." Kiko tilted her head in an affectionate gesture, and Kiyoshi didn't want to read into that. Not until tomorrow. With answers so close, he couldn't wait already, and he knew he wouldn't get any sleep tonight.

Chapter 15

Kiko and Yoshi climbed off the bus near her parents' house and strolled inside. Everything was in its proper place, except for the end table, which was now gone. The wine stain had been cleaned. Her dad was home, becoming one with the recliner, and Kiko stiffened.

Dad's face was buried in the newspaper. "Forty-five hundred. Can you believe that?" Dad lowered the paper.

"Forty-five hundred what?" Dollars in damage? Kiko couldn't afford to reimburse her parents that much. And she didn't *see* any damage left from Roger, but her parents were quick about fixing things for appearance's sake.

"Strike outs. Nolan Ryan is a god among men." Her dad looked at them both and smiled. She was nervous to bring Yoshi home, but this was the most friendly he'd ever been.

"Dad, this is my roommate, Yoshi." Kiko waved a hand awkwardly toward him, and Dad stood up. Kiko's voice caught, and she cleared her throat. "He helped me move yesterday."

"You broke that end table, huh?"

"I'm sorry, sir. It was an accident."

Dad grinned and held out his hand. Yoshi shook it. He was jittery with a nervous grin. A small part of her deep down wanted her dad to like him. Why wouldn't he? Yoshi could very well be family—*rival* family.

"Take a seat, young man. We need to have a chat." Dad gestured toward the couch.

Yoshi's eyes danced from him to her and back, and Kiko nodded encouragement. She sat on the couch, in the same place where Roger forced her to spill the wine. She shuddered. Yoshi sat next to her with plentiful space between their thighs.

"I come from a long line of Hadas. We do our best to honor our women. We treat them with respect and kindness, and we expect the men to be courageous, persistent, and honest. Like this Mr. Ryan. You don't get to forty-five hundred strikeouts by turning tail and quitting, now do you?"

Yoshi shook his head.

"We expect nothing less. Understand?"

Kiko swooped in for the rescue. "Dad, we're not..." she interrupted, trying to clarify the situation, but the words caught in her throat. She didn't stand up to Dad. She didn't correct him either. Kiko didn't know how he'd react. "We're not dating."

"What did you say your last name is?" Dad asked, ignoring her.

"I didn't, sir. Takai. Kiyoshi Takai."

Dad's face tilted thoughtfully. "We have a lot of Takais in the family. I don't recognize you, though."

"I was adopted, sir."

Dad nodded. "Well, that's a good thing. Some of those Takais—nothing but petty. You're better off."

"Uh, thanks?"

"Just remember, if you're courageous, persistent, and honest, you'll do well in life." Dad gave Yoshi a sharp stare.

"Thank you, sir." Yoshi trembled, and while she felt bad for the guy, she was glad Dad's intensity wasn't directed at her for a change.

Dad lifted his paper, and that meant the speech was over.

"Come on." She beckoned Yoshi to follow her up to her room, and he didn't hesitate. She'd never brought a guy into her room before, but since it was devoid of all her personal stuff, it didn't have any significant meaning. Inside her room, her mom had just placed the copy on the bed.

"Oh, hi, Mom," Kiko said, taken aback.

"Hey, honey." Mom greeted her with far more perkiness than usual.

"Is everything okay?"

"Just great. Here." She handed Kiko the family tree. "As requested."

Yoshi hummed at her side, waiting for the information.

"I...I have something to tell you, and I'm not sure how to do it," Mom said. That couldn't be good news. "Sweetie, your dad and I"—she glanced at Yoshi and nodded for him to stay—"we've been having difficulties for a long while. I'm sure you noticed. We've taken a lot of frustration out on each other, and that wasn't fair to you. We couldn't figure out how to reconcile our differences. But things are...well, they're a lot better now. After you moved out, we reconnected last night, if you know what I mean."

A knot formed in Kiko's stomach. She was happy for her parents, but she dreaded the rest of the conversation. Dryly, Kiko said, "That's great, Mom."

"And it was just so good... It had been so long. We missed each other. Having an empty nest rekindled an excitement for us—"

"That's enough, Mom. I got it," Kiko interrupted coldly.

Mom turned to Yoshi. "So, I just wanted to say, thank you."

Yoshi's face colored with the telltale red of embarrassment, and he nodded. He was taking this awkward conversation well. But Kiko had enough of her mom talking to her roommate like he was some romantic savior.

"We need to go," Kiko said, shaking the paper in her hand. "We have some phone calls to make." This information Yoshi had been seeking most of his life. He needed closure, but first, they needed to get out of here. The awkwardness was too much to bear.

"Sure, honey. I'll show you out."

Following her mom, Kiko grasped Yoshi's hand in support and led him down the stairs. At the door, Mom air-kissed Kiko's cheeks, and when she acknowledged Yoshi, Kiko's breath stopped in anticipation. Mom leaned in and gave him a hug. Kiko was stunned. Her parents hadn't been this cheerful in years. They were finally happy. Kiko's eyes filled with tears, and she blinked them back.

"Have fun." Mom waved.

Kiko and Yoshi stepped outside, and Mom closed the door behind them. She swiped her eyes discretely and waited until her voice was steady. "Thanks to you, my whole family seems happier."

"I am your inner peace." He recited his newspaper ad with a cheesy grin.

Kiko chuckled. "But it sucks they couldn't be happy with me around."

Yoshi rubbed her arms. "I noticed that too. I'm sorry. I know how it feels to be rejected by your family."

Kiko lifted the paper. "Let's see if you get a new one then, shall we?"

Yoshi took the paper and he studied it while they walked to the bus stop. He was silent.

"What does it say? Does any of it make sense?" she asked.

"I can't believe after all these years... Kiko." He stopped and touched her arm.

She faced him, and his eyes watered. A lump caught in her throat at his deep appreciation.

"No one has ever done anything as amazing as this. I am so thankful; you have no idea."

"I do have some idea." She crooked a smile at him, and he pulled her into a tight hug. It wasn't a romantic squeeze, just affectionate.

"So what are we?" she asked.

"I don't know. The quality isn't great." Yoshi tilted the paper into the light. "This looks like an original."

Kiko pressed her finger against the copy and followed the branching boxes of the family tree. Her name was written on the bottom of one side.

"I'm not on it," Yoshi said. "And I don't recognize any of these names. Would the Hadas alter the family tree out of spite?"

Kiko took the paper. A smudge was near the bottom. "Look at this. There's an annotation that's been erased. Let's see what we can find out. I need paper and pencil." Kiko handed the tree to Yoshi and dug in her purse. She took the paper back and sat on the bus stop bench. She lightly penciled over the dents of the annotation to reveal a name. A woman's name. "I think we need to ask her."

Chapter 16

Kiyoshi had never been more nervous in his life. He had a family tree and a name. This was the closest he'd ever been to finally getting answers. He had dreamed of how this moment would happen for years. Now it was seconds away, and panic made his heart thunder in his chest, and his stomach flipped around. Kiyoshi exhaled a deep breath.

"This is it," Kiko said while they climbed up the front porch to the townhome. It rested in the middle of an idyllic tree-lined yuppie neighborhood. A boy on a skateboard rolled by blowing bubbles with his gum. A dog barked from somewhere down the block. And a soft breeze rustled the thick maple trees in shades of red and yellow. He rubbed his sweaty palms against his pants.

Kiko gripped his hand for reassurance. "No matter what happens, we'll get through this. I don't know this lady, never met her, but she didn't sound too friendly on the phone."

At Kiko's words, a wave of strength surged through him just as the door swung wide. A forty-something woman stood with a cold expression on her face. Her gray-streaked hair was pulled into a knot on the top of her head, and her bangs were teased high. The collared shirt with a floral pattern was buttoned tight to her throat. This woman wasn't happy to hear from him, and clearly didn't want anything to do with him. He made a mistake. His body trembled, and he didn't trust his knees to keep him standing.

"You must be Kiko and Yoshi. I'm Sakura Anderson. Please come inside," she said with a dry voice.

Kiko squeezed, which he appreciated, and they followed her. Sakura gestured for them to sit on the loud-patterned couch, and she sat across from them in a coordinating accent chair. She had decor filling the walls, shelves, and end tables. This was clearly a pet-free and child-free home. A clock ticked menacingly.

Sakura held out her hand. "Let me see what you brought."

Kiko passed the woman the family tree. She looked it over with a critical eye. "Those Hadas sure know how to erase history. Don't they?"

"What do you mean?" Kiko asked.

"This isn't correct." She handed it back, and Kiko passed it to Kiyoshi.

The hopes he'd had for his family line was—worthless? "Tell us the truth," Kiyoshi demanded...politely.

The woman sighed. "Kaneyoshi Hada was a farmer, but all he thought about was smithing. He disrupted and embarrassed his family by making the sword and joining the military against his family's wishes. It's true the sword passed from father to son over the generations until, Kiko, your great-grandfather and his brother feuded over it. The names here are switched. Taro was the younger brother who was cheated of the sword, and Jiro, the older brother, had both the sword and the love of Kana. Jiro refused to return the sword. That's the truth."

Kiko's hand never left his. She asked, "How are you so certain your version of the story is true?"

Her sharp eyes darted to her, and Kiko flinched under the woman's harsh gaze.

"I have the trade agreement in writing."

Kiyoshi's lips parted. "Can we see it?"

"It's in a safe deposit box, but I have a photograph." She left the room, and Kiko and Kiyoshi exchanged surprised glances. Sakura returned and handed him the photograph. It looked newer. "Keep it. I can take a new one if I want to, which I don't."

"Uh, thanks," Kiyoshi said.

Kiko leaned forward to read the tiny print in the photo. "It looks real," she said.

Dearest brother Jiro,

With great respect I shall offer an exchange intent upon making both parties agreeable. It is offered herein that I, Taro, the next of kin and true owner of the katana forged by Kaneyoshi Hada, will trade such a valuable instrument for Kana Okino's hand in marriage. This agreement is binding upon Okino's agreement. This arrangement as set forth will ensure agreeableness to both parties. If either

party determines an err has been made, then
the arrangement is nullified.

Kindly address your response.

Yours,
Taro Hada

The ancient print was hardly legible, but it was there. "I wonder if one side of the family reversed the truth purposely to continue the feud," Kiyoshi speculated.

"Sounds likely," Kiko said. "The way my dad told the story was heartfelt. He believed it to be true, so somewhere along the lines, someone wanted to stir up drama."

And that led Kiyoshi to ask, "Why was your name erased from the family tree?"

"It's because of you," Sakura said flatly. Kiyoshi didn't know this woman, but he felt that stab through the heart at those curt words. It wasn't easy for him to sit here under her scrutinizing gaze. He hadn't received the warm welcome wagon from his family he'd always envisioned.

"Care to elaborate?" Kiko asked.

"I married into the Takai family, but my husband and I didn't want children. When he deployed to Afghanistan, I made a mistake with your father, Kiyoshi. My husband and I couldn't agree with a solution to the problem. So, we quietly divorced, freeing me from the drama of the Takais, and I gave you up."

Kiyoshi stared down his birth mother, and as he'd suspected, he was never wanted—a mistake. He couldn't understand how anyone could give up their child. But how could someone who clearly wasn't struggling to survive do that? Did she really believe giving him up would've given him a better life? Her attitude against him made him believe his adoptive family was better after all.

"As to your question, Kiyoshi, you were incorrectly assumed to be a Takai, and because of the rift it caused the family, you were named after Kaneyoshi Hada."

The legendary disruptive embarrassment of the family. How honorable. Kiyoshi swallowed back the cotton in his throat. "Who was the man who gave my parents the sword?"

"I presume that was your grandfather. He didn't know you weren't of his blood, and he passed away believing you were."

His grandfather cared, but would the man's opinion have changed had he known Kiyoshi's true parentage? Now he'd never know. "And my father? He didn't want me either?"

Sakura shrugged. "Never saw him again. Couldn't tell you his name. As I said, the pregnancy was a problem for me and my husband to resolve."

"He never knew," Kiyoshi said on a breath.

Sakura didn't answer that. How despicable could one person be?

"I was adopted by Takais. That couldn't have been a coincidence."

"True, you're not a Takai at all, but a relative of my ex-husband's decided to raise you anyway. Not out of obligation to the family, but because they simply couldn't conceive. I believe we're done here." Sakura stood, mouth set grim.

Kiyoshi could hardly find the strength to stand, but Kiko helped him to his feet, and she thanked the woman for her time.

On the porch, Kiko embraced him, and he fell into her arms. Kiko's hand rubbed his back, just as he'd done for her, and he sucked back a sob.

"I'm sorry that didn't go the way you wanted. I couldn't imagine cherishing that sword for years as the sole connection to your family, only to find out you were lied to, and have that connection ripped away."

"At least now I know."

"There's a silver lining in all storms. How about we bring the last of my boxes to our house?"

Liking the sound of 'our', Kiyoshi pulled back, and he smiled. "There's one other silver lining."

"What's that?" Kiko asked.

"We aren't blood relations at all."

"That's actually a huge relief," Kiko said.

Kiyoshi agreed, but asked, "Why is that?"

"It makes what we did okay instead of awkward and gross."

"Gross? You found me gross?"

Kiko smiled. "Not at all. Just the idea we might've been related was gross. I rather enjoyed everything you did, especially that thing with your tongue."

"I can do that again, anytime you want."

Kiko playfully swatted him on the arm, and Kiyoshi beamed with pride and affection that he'd never felt for anyone else. She helped him in ways no one else had, and she even brought him the answers he'd been searching for. Kiko was perfect. "You're amazing," he said.

"You're not too bad yourself," Kiko said.

That weird warm feeling? That was hope, and Kiyoshi grabbed onto it like a lifeline.

"Wait until you see what I can do with a stack of boxes."

Kiko grinned, and her cheeks burned red. "I'll admit, you have me curious."

Kiyoshi wanted her mouth, her body, and her soul. "Let's go home."

They boarded the bus, and he believed he was better off without his birth mother. He'd thought she would restore a missing piece of him with the visit, but Kiyoshi realized the missing piece of his heart had already been filled. Kiko made him whole. While she sat next to him on the ambling bus, Kiyoshi blurted what he wanted most, "Go out with me."

Kiko flinched. Her mouth opened and closed.

Kiyoshi added before she could reject him again, "One night. My treat. If it doesn't work out, we'll remain roommates...and friends. No weirdness between us."

Kiko blinked and touched his hand. "I'd like that."

Kiyoshi tried not to whoop with excitement. Finally, things were looking up.

Chapter 17

Fluorescent lights in the empty mall corridor flicked off one by one. Closing time in twenty minutes. Kiko finished folding the last of the women's shirts that customers had scattered throughout the day. With midterms coming up, she took the quiet opportunity to talk to herself. There were many research methods, and a few of them—surveys, case studies, and experimental studies—were easy to remember. The harder ones—correlational research, quasi-experiments, and others in her textbook—were trickier to remember. And soon she'd have to pick one for her own class project. She invented and recited mnemonics to help.

Being Yoshi's roommate and having his respect and the quiet she needed, her dream to help people navigate marriage and family relationships was within grasp. Only one and a half semesters left until graduation. Then she wouldn't have to worry about regular tuition bills, and she could finally help people be happy.

All she'd wanted was a break from her schoolwork with a simple one-night stand, and she'd scored huge on that front, but Yoshi was so much more than she imagined. He was sweet, devoted, and fiercely loyal. And after discovering they weren't related, a dam to her heart broke free. And that was why she'd agreed to go out with him. She didn't want to fight their attraction any longer.

"Good evening, Kiko," a familiar voice purred, startling her.

Kiko smoothed the shirt and turned. Yoshi stood before her with a fabulous crooked smile, and her chest swelled with warmth and pride. She'd made the right decision. She could save troubled couples and have her own slice of happiness at the same time.

Off Yoshi's shoulder stood another man she hadn't met before. He was stunning—tall and lean like Yoshi, but with sandy blond hair and soft green eyes. He wore sleek black dress pants and a striped button-up shirt rolled up to his elbows. Kiko rubbed her palms on her pants and blinked like a deer trapped in a car's headlights. He was intimidatingly beautiful, but the stranger smiled with friendly eyes.

"This is my best friend, Eric Woodson," Yoshi said.

Eric held out his hand to her, and as she shook it, her heart skipped a beat. An imaginary zap of electricity tore through his touch, and her hand trembled. She didn't know what was wrong with her. Kiko pulled her hand back.

"Nice to finally meet you," Eric said with a warm smile. "I've heard all about you."

"I hope not too much," she replied with a playful friendliness and darted a look at Yoshi. Surely he didn't share details to more guys, after Roger attacked her for it.

Yoshi asked, "Any chance we can steal you for a while?" He stuffed his hands in the front pockets of his dark wash jeans, and he wore a sweater over a turtleneck. He was so handsome. She wanted to climb up under his shirt and trail kisses all over his bare skin. She checked the clock on the back wall.

"Steal me? Why?"

"Date night is tonight," Yoshi said, eyes sparkling with excitement.

Kiko's gaze tracked to Eric. A group date? She was wholly underdressed and unprepared. "Tonight? I'm wearing work clothes, and I'm on the clock for five more minutes."

"You look great. We'll be waiting right here," Yoshi said.

"No, you won't," a deep woman's voice boomed behind her. Kiko's manager stepped forward, arms carrying a stack of folded shirts. "Store's closed. Go wait outside the gate, please."

Yoshi nodded and smiled. "Yes, ma'am." Yoshi and Eric strolled out to the benches splitting the corridor of storefronts.

Kiko accepted the stack from her manager and carefully positioned them where they belonged. "Can I leave now?"

"You're done tonight. Go. Enjoy your men." Her manager winked, and heat rushed up her cheeks.

"It's not like that."

Her manager made a dismissive noise, not believing her. Kiko scooted away to the back room, punched out, and retrieved her purse from her mini locker. When she reached the benches, the pair of handsome men stood. Yoshi hooked his arm around her waist.

"Where are we going tonight?" she asked and leaned her head against his shoulder.

"Knock some pins around."

Kiko snorted. "You mean you two will knock some pins around. I'm always good for testing the gutter system, but the good news is, none have failed so far. They don't call me the gutter ball queen for nothing."

"Aww, you can't be that bad," Eric said.

Kiko lifted her head from Yoshi's shoulder, and a ball of nerves swirled in her belly when she made eye contact with Eric. "Clearly you haven't seen me wield heavy balls." And when the words left her mouth, she pinched her lips between her teeth. Idiot.

Eric laughed. "I do know from personal experience Yoshi's got a pair. I've seen how he fights, and I heard how he took down Roger. That guy's in a class all by himself, and to do something like that, well, Yoshi has major *cojones*."

Instead of picking on Kiko, Eric praised Yoshi. And at once, she relaxed. Yoshi might've had terrible family and a worse 'friend', but at least he had one good person in his life.

"Are you saying you want Yoshi to help protect you?" she teased as they pushed through the mall doors.

Yoshi's chest rumbled by her ear with a chuckle, and they made their way through the nearly-empty parking lot. The crisp air sent a small chill through her short sleeves, but it felt refreshing and alive.

"On the contrary," Eric said. "We're going out tonight to have unrestrained fun, and since it's the local hotspot, I'm tagging along to keep you safe. Strangely enough, after all this *cojones* talk, I don't think I'm needed at all."

"You're coming," Yoshi said seriously, and that got Kiko's attention.

"Are you expecting Roger to be there?"

"No, not at all," Yoshi said, rubbing her back. "But my homeboy and I haven't had a night out in a while, and with your help on the rent, I'm now a little less broke, so tonight's my treat. Besides, I figured with all your studying, you needed a break, and I'd rather you join me in my plan than repeat yours." Yoshi gave her a possessive squeeze.

The last time she'd needed a school break, she wound up in Yoshi's bed, and couch, and kitchen counter, and shower...for one night only. But the one night didn't stick.

Kiko glanced at Eric, but he kept his eyes on the parking lot surface. No one wanted to hear about their best friend's bedroom conquests. She didn't blame him. "Well, if it's anything to you, I'd rather not hear that man's name ever again."

"After what you went through," Eric said, "I don't blame you."

Yoshi squeezed her shoulders. "Eric and I will make sure he-who-will-not-be-named never harms you again, understand?"

"He's right," Eric said fiercely. "Both of us are competent fighters, just like he-who-will-not-be-named. You have my word."

Kiko couldn't help a warm smile. They wanted her to feel comfortable and safe, and it worked. The three of them approached the lone vehicle in this area of the parking lot. This wasn't Yoshi's black company car, but it was a luxury vehicle she hadn't expected. Eric opened the back for her. "Climb in you two crazy kids, and let's have some fun."

Kiko climbed in first. "I can't wait."

Yoshi climbed in next to her, and Eric took the driver's seat.

She never felt safer than between these two men.

Chapter 18

Every parking space at the bowling alley had been taken, and people packed the interior. The owner installed automatic scoring computers recently, so everyone wanted to test them out. Bright lights lit up the lanes, and crashes of pins echoed every few seconds. In between the murmurs of people chatting, cheers came from different places, and flashes of cameras dotted the busy crowd. Off to the side was an arcade and a bar with billiards, darts, and food. A short wait for a lane to open allowed them enough time to buy drinks and rent shoes, Yoshi's treat. Kiko had picked a small ten-pound ball, figuring she'd be able to throw it down the lane half the night without killing her arm.

Kiko sipped from her soda, while waiting her turn. Shuffling carefully on the approach, Yoshi hooked his arm and launched his ball toward the pins in a practiced curving path, earning yet another strike. He excelled at everything that required hand strength. Her cheeks heated, and she bit her lip to hide her thoughts from showing on her face.

Turned out Eric Woodson was just as skilled at bowling as Yoshi, and just as fun to watch. Hey, she was dating a guy, she wasn't dead. The curvature of his body and the strength of his arms were better than watching television. And when he turned around, celebrating his next strike, Kiko's gaze met his. Kiko wished she'd brought a girl for Eric. Kiko cared very much for Yoshi, but having a visible barrier between her and Eric would've been a nice reminder to keep her thoughts where they belonged, because right now, they kept gliding into places they didn't belong. Maybe she was just so grateful for both of them that her affections wanted to show them both how she felt.

"You're up, short stuff," Eric said, sitting next to her.

A flush of heat tore through her. Kiko cleared her throat and gripped her ball. On the approach, she pretended to line up the ball with the pins as if she knew what she was doing. She'd already warned them she sucked, but for their sake and the fun of the evening, she really tried. Kiko launched her ball down the lane and when three pins tipped over, she covered her mouth with her hands. Holy shit. Her streak of good luck hadn't run out yet, and Eric and Yoshi were right. She was having a great time.

And she didn't need the bumpers. *Take that, 'gutter ball queen' title!*

Kiko returned to her seat between Yoshi and Eric, her own personal bodyguards. Yoshi slipped a disposable one-ten camera out of his back pocket and held it up in front of the three of them. "Say cheese."

The men hugged her, and Kiko's heart pounded hard.

"Stick your tongue out," Eric said.

She faced him, and yes, his tongue peeked out between his lips. Kiko's nerves eased, and she copied him.

They all made a humming noise while the camera flashed in their eyes. Laughter erupted again. Her cheeks were hurting.

"My turn." She held out her hand for the camera and Yoshi gave it up. She stood and snapped a couple pictures of the best friends, and Yoshi reclaimed it. "Your turn. My two most favorite people need a shot together."

Kiko sat next to Eric, and her breathing was hitched and ragged.

Yoshi gestured for them to lean in. "Scoot closer."

She tried.

"Closer," Yoshi repeated with a smile.

Kiko shifted another inch.

"Hug. You can do this, Kiko."

Eric's strong arm wrapped over her shoulders and pressed her against him. Kiko's thunderous heart echoed in her ears, and her hand trembled. Where should she put it? On her thigh or was that too formal? On his? No, that was too personal, right? She settled for the edge of the chair.

"Smile," Yoshi ordered, sticking the viewfinder up against his eye. He snapped another picture and cranked the advancing wheel over for the next shot.

Kiko looked at Eric just as the flash lit up his eyes. Why was she such a mess over Yoshi's friend? She needed a breather.

"And now it's full. I can't wait to get these developed." Yoshi pocketed the camera and took up his seat next to her. "Eric, your turn."

And there it was. In Yoshi's arms, she watched Eric plan out his move. Kiko couldn't remember having so much fun before. Not even at high school dances or friends' sleepovers. Something about Yoshi just reached down into her marrow. She was excited for the images to get developed too. She would hang a couple on their wall, no matter how silly they turned out.

"I gotta run to the little boys' room. Be right back." Yoshi got up and shared a glance with Eric, and the blond nodded.

She could only guess it was their agreement to keep her safe, which now seemed like overkill, and the fact that they were still taking it so seriously was ridiculous. But Kiko didn't look a gift horse in the mouth.

Eric finished his turn and approached her. He didn't remind her it was her turn, but Kiko got up anyway and picked up her ball. Repeating her last attempt, she lined the ball up with the pins. Kiko swung and released, knowing Eric was watching her—not at all distracted by Yoshi. The ball thumped harder than she preferred, but it didn't go into the gutter. She leaned as the ball rolled off course, slowly, and knocked one pin over. Kiko smiled.

When she turned around, Eric leaned back in the curved plastic seat, arms stretched wide and resting on the tops of the chairs. He watched the electronic scoreboard's animations above him. Kiko sat next to him, resuming her seat, even though she could've picked any other open chair. She didn't want him to know how he affected her.

"So, you and Yoshi?" Eric said.

"Yep."

"You've given him a gift that no one else could've, closure on the past that's always haunted him. He's..." Eric looked at her with appreciation. "He's finally happy. I've never seen him like this before."

"Thanks." She didn't know what else to say to the compliment.

"And you're living together?"

"Yep."

"That's fast."

Kiko felt the need to defend herself. "We were roommates. It's a mutually beneficial agreement."

"Really?" Eric's brow lifted. "Is there a contract signed in blood?"

Kiko frowned. "What?"

"My dad always talks about contracts like your signature is your soul. 'Mutually beneficial' is a phrase I hear a lot, because someone is always getting more out of the relationship than the other. He fights to make it fair. It's his whole life."

Kiko's interest was piqued. "Your parents must have a strong marriage."

"They do. How did you figure?"

"I have a special interest in marriage."

Eric's clear discomfort had him shifting in his seat.

Kiko relaxed seeing the unease shift from her to him. She quickly added, "It's my major. I'm going to be a marriage and family counselor."

Eric smiled. "We can never have enough of those. So, how are you enjoying the night so far?"

"It's fun."

"You're not thinking about flash cards and study guides, are you?" Eric teased. "I heard you're something of a bookworm."

"Studying is part of graduating, so under those terms, yes, I'm a 'bookworm,'" Kiko said dryly. She'd rather be a bookworm than a gutter ball queen. "And pretty soon I have to start my class project, so I'll be a book *worshiper*."

"I'm majoring in finance," Eric said. "Our projects are spreadsheets with colorful graphs. What's yours? Dissecting a couple in mediation?"

Kiko chuckled. "Spread *sheets* sounds either really dull or really exciting."

Eric tilted his head thoughtfully. "I never thought of it that way, but I like your thinking."

Heat flushed up her cheeks. "I need to study a willing participant and ask questions about his interpersonal relationships." *His?* Kiko just had to specify 'his' like a Freudian slip, but she didn't mean it. "For my project, I mean."

"You should study me. I'm fascinating."

Kiko laughed and a jolt a energy surged through her. "Says the guy who loves spreadsheets."

Eric laughed, a deep rumble from his strong chest.

She needed a distraction. The more time she spent with him, the more confused she got.

A loud voice turned heads in the crowded bowling alley. Why wasn't Yoshi back yet? Did he eat something bad tonight?

Through the crowd, a large blond monster approached the lanes and scanned the area. Ice slithered down her spine. Suddenly lightheaded, she cupped a hand over her eyes to hide her face.

"What's wrong, Kiko?" Eric asked.

"He's here."

Eric's posture stiffened, and he craned his neck around on high alert. When he spotted what she feared, he touched her thigh. "I'm right here, and the place is busy. He won't see us, but if he does, Yoshi will be right back. We got this, okay? Just ignore him. Can you do that?"

Kiko nodded. "Yeah, I think so." Every time she thought of Roger, she only pictured the monster's skewed face while his iron-like hands forced themselves on her. Kiko trembled, and her heart raced, but she made herself small so he wouldn't see her. Now she wanted Eric to distract her. "You're a kendo practitioner with Yoshi. Who's the better fighter?" A distraction and a reassurance.

Eric grinned. "That's not the basis of the art, but I understand what you mean. I suppose you'll get differing answers between us, but I can assure you, I'm a fourth-*dan*."

"And Yoshi?"

"First-*dan*, but in his defense, it costs money to test. That doesn't mean his skills are that much lower than mine."

"And Roger?"

"Kiko," Eric said softly, touching her arm. "Don't worry about him. He won't hurt you again. Yoshi and I won't let him."

Kiko nodded, fighting the terrifying images from barraging her mind and ruining her night.

"Good evening, Kiko," a gravelly voice reached her ear, and at once her blood ran cold.

Roger.

Overhead, the terrifying brute leaned against the railing. Kiko flew from her seat toward the lanes, and as promised, Eric rushed to her side.

"Leave us alone," Eric said.

Roger's hands went up in surrender, and he grinned casually. His friendliness was a stark contrast to what she last remembered, but she wasn't changing her stance. Eric was safe; Roger was not. "Whoa, whoa. It's okay," Roger said with a chuckle. "I won't hurt you, and I'm not even going to comment on you two. Kiko, can we chat?"

Eric shifted in front of her. "Stay away from her, Rodg. You're not welcome here."

"Hey, it's a free country. Calm down, Woodson. I only came to apologize."

Eric stayed, arms crossed over his puffed chest, and Roger sauntered down the carpeted steps.

Kiko thought of the only thing she could to stop him. "You can't be down here without bowling shoes."

"Kiko, the rule follower. Except when you shack up with a guy you hardly know, and now you're making the moves on his best friend. What would Yoshi think?"

"He's in the restroom," Eric said.

"Is that so?" Roger stopped near the ball return.

Eric stiffened at her side. He might be whatever a *dan* was, but he never said if Roger was ranked higher. All she could do was judge their size, and she wasn't convinced Eric had the ability to best Roger if the need arose.

"Can we sit?" Roger asked.

"Whatever you need to say, you can do it from over there," Eric said.

Kiko agreed.

"Fine." Roger cleared his throat. "I don't know what came over me that day. I think I just wanted you so bad, and I don't take rejection well."

"You have a girlfriend," Kiko interrupted, grasping at straws for something to make him leave.

"So does Woodson. Apparently that doesn't stop you, Kiko," Roger said.

Eric had a girlfriend? That was good news, but Kiko couldn't focus on that right now. No, Roger had to slip in another insult. "Apparently it doesn't stop you either," she retorted.

"Uh, no," Roger said. "Of course not, but at least I own up to it. No one's ever rejected me before, and I don't know. I didn't take it well."

She didn't know what to tell Roger, but she wasn't going to forgive him. Her tongue was glued to the roof of her mouth, and her limbs froze. The pins crackled and scattered down the lanes alongside them. Cheers roared. Everyone was having a blast, and she felt like she was in a nightmare. Where was Yoshi?

Kiko didn't want to antagonize Roger, but she needed to stand her ground. "That's not an excuse. You have no right to touch anyone without permission."

Roger darted her with daggers, and finally, bursting from the crowd, Yoshi zipped up to Roger's face with an aggressive posture. "Back away from my girlfriend."

Roger chuckled. "You should be telling that to Woodson."

Yoshi didn't face them, ignoring Roger's unfounded accusation. If a fight broke out, all four of them would be ejected from the building, and the four of them left alone in the parking lot with no witnesses was a bad idea. Eric approached Yoshi, having sensed the same thing, and he pressed a hand against Yoshi's chest.

Double teamed, Roger's hands went skyward. "I just came to explain. No harm, no foul."

"You can do that without being so close. Back up," Yoshi said, refusing to back down from Roger's bulk, and Eric remained in place too, ready at a moment's notice to do whatever necessary to keep Kiko safe—even if it was to calm Yoshi.

"Alright, alright. Take a chill pill, guys." Roger still didn't move, but he glared at Kiko. His words might've been his attempt at reconciliation and apology, but Kiko was still unnerved by him. Yoshi being friendly with Roger made her want to vomit. She never liked the guy, even before he attacked her.

"Keep your hands to yourself, otherwise I'll have to teach you right from wrong like your mother never did," Yoshi spat his warning.

"Both of us will," Eric added.

Roger lifted his hands in surrender and retreated, but Kiko could tell there was unfinished business between the friends.

Chapter 19

WEEKS PASSED, AND KIKO and Yoshi had been living together and having fun the entire time. He'd been pulling overtime hours lately, working toward a promotion, and trying to make a better life for them. He'd promised to finish emptying the spare bedroom for her private office soon. Kiko had assured him she didn't mind. She had her career to focus on too, and Kiko took advantage of the extra quiet to study for finals—no private office needed.

But tonight was a special night. Yoshi was taking her out, but the only clue he'd given her was to wear something nice. So, did that mean cocktail dress or just no jeans? He wouldn't say, so she rummaged in her half of the closet, and played it safe with a black pencil skirt and a ruffled blouse with a bold magenta-and-turquoise floral pattern. She poked thick plastic turquoise hoops through her pierced ears and crimped her elbow-length hair. As long as they weren't chasing chickens on a farm, she'd be okay.

"All set, honey?" Yoshi leaned against the door frame of their bedroom.

In the mirror over her dresser, Kiko dabbed her lips with pink gloss. She closed the tiny container and rubbed her lips together. "I am now." She smiled at him, and butterflies kicked around her stomach.

"You look beautiful." With his beaming smile, his affectionate eyes crinkled at the corners.

"You're pretty hot yourself." She was in awe the gorgeous model from Blockbuster wanted her. He was perfect in so many ways, and he was stunning in black dress pants and a striped button up with a coordinating tie. At least she wasn't overdressed. No chickens tonight, unless they were on the menu.

"Let's go." Yoshi beckoned her to join him and she gripped his arm. Outside at the curb, a black limo waited, and a driver stood ramrod straight next to the back door, gloved hands clasped neatly together.

Kiko's jaw dropped open. "What's this?"

"We aren't taking the bus tonight." Yoshi led her down to the waiting limo and the driver opened the backseat door for her.

Kiko slid inside and Yoshi followed her. The driver closed the door and got behind the wheel. From a small window in the partition, the driver said, "Good evening, miss. Enjoy your ride."

"Thank you," she said.

The partition closed, and the driver pulled the ostentatious car away from the curb. Streetlights flashed as they rolled through town, and Yoshi's leg bounced with nervousness.

"Where are we going?" she asked.

Yoshi squeezed her hand. "It's a surprise."

Kiko smiled. "I got that, but you seem on edge. What's wrong?"

"Nothing," he croaked and cleared his throat. "There's absolutely nothing wrong." Yoshi kissed her knuckles, but his leg kept bouncing.

The limo stopped curbside at a fancy restaurant, way too far out of their budget.

"Are you sure this is the right place?"

Yoshi beamed. "I'm sure."

The driver appeared at the back of the car, and he opened her door. He escorted her by the hand onto the curb, and Yoshi followed. Before they walked inside, Yoshi tipped the driver and collected her in his arms. The limo driver bowed. "Thank you, sir. Have a lovely evening."

Yoshi nodded to the man, and the driver returned to the car and pulled away in a swift and practiced sequence.

"That was different," Kiko said.

"Different?" Yoshi repeated. "It's a special ride for a special date."

"Did you close a big sale?" she asked playfully.

"I did," he said with a nod and opened the restaurant's door for her. Lights dangled low overhead, and dark mahogany walls and accents gave off a sophisticated vibe. Black leather booths lined the perimeter, and water trickled down a brick accent wall. Kiko's eyes widened. She was a ramen noodle and Pop-Tart kind of girl, not a Michelin connoisseur. Her butterflies were not playing nice. How was she supposed to eat when her stomach was swirling?

Yoshi stopped them at the hostess podium. A young lady greeted them by name and brought them to a semi-private booth near the back. A pair of menus and a roll of silverware awaited them. Yoshi gestured for her to take a seat, and he sat across from her. After a short greeting, the hostess left.

"Must've been a big one," Kiko said.

"A big what?"

"Sale?" Kiko asked. How did he forget already?

"It was."

"Wow, that's great news. I'm proud of you," Kiko said, excited for Yoshi.

"Can I get you anything to start?" the server asked. Kiko opened the menu, and her brows popped at the prices. Celebrate, indeed. He must've sold a mansion, or a penthouse suite.

Perspiration shined on Yoshi's brow. His fumbling fingers dropped the menu on the table, but he quickly retrieved it. Something was off with him tonight. Why would a big sale make him nervous?

Yoshi cleared his throat. "Bring out the bubbly and a basket of your finest cheese curds." For a split second, it looked like Yoshi winked at the server, but with his bundle of nerves, he probably had an eyelash bugging him. "And I'll have the surf 'n turf."

Kiko skimmed the menu and ordered something small. Just how big was this sale?

The server took their menus and rushed off.

Kiko said, "Are you going to tell me about it?"

"About what?" he croaked again.

"Your big sale."

"Right. About that..." Yoshi trailed off. "There wasn't actually any special sale."

"Wait, so how can we afford this?" Kiko meant 'we' because they were both responsible for the rent. She loved her new home, and she didn't want to lose it because of rash decisions.

"I've been saving for weeks just for tonight."

Kiko tilted her head. What was so special about tonight? Did she miss an important date? A holiday? She couldn't think of anything.

The server returned, pushing a metal cart over with a stainless steel pail filled with ice and a bottle of champagne. Next to the pail rested a pair of glass flutes. And on the lower shelf, a round covered serving dish waited. A celebration for something Kiko couldn't remember. Well, shit. She wracked her brain trying to remember anything about today, but she came up empty, and that made her feel like an ungrateful ass.

The server poured both glasses and set them in front of her and Yoshi. She nodded and left.

Yoshi waited to take a drink, and Kiko didn't know what she was supposed to do.

Yoshi cleared his throat and lifted one of the flutes in a toast. Kiko copied him. "To the woman in front of me: Kiko Hada." He sipped, and Kiko followed. Taking his lead, she set hers down when he did, and his eyes became glassy. Yoshi collected her hands in his. All of this to thank her? Yoshi's thumbs rubbed her hands. "You found me when I was lost. You healed me when I was broken." His voice quavered.

His beautiful words left her speechless, and her eyes watered.

"You complete me," Yoshi continued. "Without you, I am a shadow of who I was meant to be. I love you so very much." His voice broke. "I knew you were the one since half-way through *Indiana Jones and the Temple of Doom*, which I did rewind and return."

Kiko's breath hitched. Was this really happening?

"Kiko, will you do me the honor of giving me your hand in marriage?" His hands squeezed hers in silent pleading.

Kiko's chest squeezed. She'd thought he'd closed a big sale, and she expected grand promises from big numbers—a promotion, a new house, their first car. Things she didn't need, but thought he wanted. Kiko hadn't expected a proposal. Her vision became wavy as tears flowed over. One hand released hers, and Yoshi produced a velvety black box between his fingers, opened and sparkling under the restaurant lights. The amazing ring must've cost him a month's salary. It was almost too much to accept. She smiled through her tears. "I love you, Yoshi."

The man of her dreams waited.

She'd never been happier, and she couldn't imagine a better life. "And of course, I'll marry you."

Yoshi leaned over the table, and brought his lips to hers. Nearby customers cheered their kiss, and with all the attention, Kiko smiled through the kiss, which ended quickly.

The server returned and uncovered the serving dish—a small round cake with fresh flowers and piped frosting. She served a slice of cake to each of them. "Congratulations."

"Thank you," Yoshi said, pushing the jeweled ring on her finger.

"I love you," Kiko said.

"I will love you until forever," Yoshi said and snaked both his hands across the table to hold hers. Yoshi's sleeve bumped a flute of champagne. It tipped over and splashed their plates and flooded the table and dripped onto her skirt.

Yoshi froze, his face red as a tomato, and he waited for her reaction. Good thing she hadn't worn the cocktail dress. Her heart soared with love, and nothing could spoil it—not even sticky bubbly. Kiko laughed. "I hope that wasn't a bad omen."

The server, who hadn't gotten far, returned to clean up the table. She apologized unnecessarily.

Yoshi smiled in relief and kissed her knuckles. "I don't believe in bad omens. We're just being tested."

"Did I pass?"

"With flying colors."

With a new table cloth, fresh silverware, and new slices of cake, they each savored a bite. They were getting married. Soon Kiko would graduate, and Yoshi was working on getting a promotion. Everything was just perfect.

Chapter 20

KIYOSHI'S FOCUS WAS SOLELY on Kiko, and his opponent was going to win again, only this time, it was Eric Woodson, and Kiyoshi wasn't ashamed to lose to his best friend. Kiyoshi's feet shifted, and he spun and struck, but Eric dodged the blow, and their *shinais* locked at the hilts. Leaning close, Eric said, "Perhaps you should take the rest of class off."

"What? Why?" Kiyoshi said. "You're only up one point."

Through the grate of his *men*, Eric said, "Your focus is in the toilet, and I don't blame you. If I was marrying her, I'd be a blubbering mess too."

Kiyoshi ripped free and spun. "I'm not a blubbering mess."

"No offense intended, Yoshi. I just don't want something bad to happen while your head isn't here." Eric darted in for a point against Kiyoshi's *kote*, but he lifted his forearms to counter. The force still knocked Kiyoshi's balance off, and he stumbled back. Eric stared, point taken, literally and figuratively.

"I'm not quitting. I've been pulling late nights at the office, cold calling to drum up clients."

"Is it working?"

"I have a few showings this week."

"Congrats, Yoshi. Sounds like things are going well for you, except this match." Eric's *shinai* struck Kiyoshi's *men* in a laser-quick flash. "Point."

So maybe Eric was right. Yoshi stepped back, the match having ended, and they both bowed to each other.

"Hey, man," Roger said, and Kiyoshi righted himself. Eric stayed, waiting for the all clear. After his half-assed attempt at a Roger-style apology, Kiyoshi didn't trust him.

"Hey," Yoshi said coldly.

"Can we talk—just you and me?" Roger asked, eyes flashing to Eric and back.

"We have nothing more to talk about." Kiyoshi removed his *men*. He'd barely contained himself when Roger's smugness strutted through Main Street Realty every day toward his lofty office. Even now, after an hour of sparring with Eric to burn off the adrenaline coursing through Yoshi's veins, he wanted to fight.

While other pairs sparred around them, ignoring the drama, Eric stared daggers at Roger. In moments, the *sensei* would come over and intervene, likely lie down another scolding.

Roger said, "I only need a few minutes."

Kiyoshi didn't want to lose his dojo. It was the only thing that made him feel like he belonged somewhere in the world. "Follow me." Kiyoshi moved toward the locker room. If Roger was going to waste his time, it would be while Kiyoshi was doing something worthwhile. Eric stayed by his side, and Kiyoshi appreciated the support. Eric was the best.

Kiyoshi pushed through the locker room door with Roger on his tail and Eric as backup. Pungent sweaty gym clothes stung his nose.

"I'm sorry," Roger said to his back.

"That's not good enough." Kiyoshi stopped at his locker, spun the dial of his padlock, and opened the door. The last face he wanted to see was Roger's. They had been buddies for a couple years—in and outside of the dojo, but Roger blew it all to pieces, because he attacked a woman, a woman Kiyoshi was going to marry.

"I'll be nearby," Eric said and patted Kiyoshi on the shoulder. Kiyoshi acknowledged him with a nod, and Eric walked around to the next bank of lockers.

"Hear me out, okay? I don't know what came over me. Not that it's an excuse, but Jessica dumped me, and I was lost and broken. I needed to feel the touch of a female."

"You're right." Kiyoshi slipped into his pants and shirt. He would shower after he got home. Being near Roger any longer than necessary made his skin itch. Roger beamed, so Kiyoshi finished his statement. "It's absolutely not an excuse. There's never an excuse to lay your hands on a woman. I thought better of you, Roger, but I was wrong. I'd never been more stupid in my life. I should never have introduced you to her."

"I get it. You feel guilty." Roger raked his fingers into the teased lengths of his hair, not in concern or worry, but vanity. "You have to understand, Jessica, she was just something special. The other day, right out of the blue, she calls me a few names and slams the door in my face. We were supposed to, you know..." Roger made unnecessary obscene gestures. "And she left me hanging.

I just snapped. My neck still kills from that end table, man, but I deserved it. I deserve it all over again. If I let Kiko slap me in the face, can we all be chill again?"

Kiyoshi studied Roger's intentions with skepticism.

"A big one, a small one. Her choice. I don't care," Roger added with a hopeful tone at Kiyoshi's hesitation.

Kiyoshi squinted.

Roger's features eased as he sensed Kiyoshi's barrier cracking. "You can help her. Make sure she does the job right. Hey, it might be a week before I wake up."

Kiyoshi cracked a smile. Damn him. "She slaps you as hard as she wants, and I get a freebie with no strings attached."

"Deal. I knew you'd come around. Seriously, you both can give me a beating, and I won't resist."

Eric slammed his locker door unnecessarily loudly, and it echoed through the room.

Roger's meaty hand landed on Kiyoshi's shoulder in an invitation to hug, and Kiyoshi reluctantly clapped backs with him. Roger wasn't fixed, he wasn't changed, but deep down, Kiyoshi believed, in Roger's own Roger way, that he was sorry.

"Seriously though," the hulking blond said. "How is Kiko doing? Is she still shook up?"

Remembering her trembling in his arms and fighting back sobs made the anger surge through Kiyoshi. He stabbed a finger in Roger's face. "Never touch her again, or I'll kill you." Kiyoshi meant every word. He lowered his finger and said, "But I suppose she's alright. She doesn't want to talk about it."

"Message received loud and clear, man. Has she mentioned me?"

Kiyoshi thought for a minute. Unless Roger was standing directly in her view, Kiko never mentioned him. "No."

Roger shifted his feet, and Kiyoshi slung his equipment bag over his shoulder and re-locked his locker. Roger stood between him and the exit.

"Have you talked to her lately?" Roger asked.

"This morning. Why?"

"Roommates in passing? I bet you too see a lot of each other."

"Of course we do." Kiyoshi's tone sharpened in warning. He didn't like Roger mentioning Kiko, but the tone he used put him back on high alert.

"Man, she is just so..." he trailed off, and his hands made unintelligible motions, which Kiyoshi believed would be offensive if Roger completed them. "I mean, since you're roommates, maybe you could put in a good word for me. You know, play up the apology and smooth things over. Of course, this would be after the epic slap, which, there's a chance I might actually like it."

Kiyoshi held back wanting to pummel the large blond right here, right now. "Don't talk about my fiancée like that. This is your last warning." Kiyoshi didn't mean to tell him, honestly. He wanted to keep his and Kiko's exciting day far away from Roger, but it popped out as a gloat.

"What?" Roger barked his question. "You hardly know her. How can you marry your roommate so soon?" Roger's face flushed red.

Kiyoshi had no idea why Roger would care at all, but he didn't want to talk to Roger any longer. He readjusted the strap on his shoulder and shifted to get around Roger's bulk. "I don't have to explain anything to you."

"But—" Roger paused and blew out a frustrated breath. He moved to block the way out. "Hear me out. I think you're making a mistake."

Fury pulsed through Kiyoshi's veins. His hands balled into fists, his tone a warning, "Get out of my way."

Roger didn't back down. Kiyoshi dropped his equipment bag to the floor with a dull thump. A strong hand pushed back on Kiyoshi's chest. Eric got between them, but instead of standing on his side to warn Roger away, Eric faced Kiyoshi. "Cool off, Takai. You don't want to do this."

Kiyoshi stared down his best friend, fists aching to slug Roger in the jaw. "I do. That asshole has gone too far."

Eric darted a warning look over Kiyoshi's shoulder, and Roger stomped out of the locker room. Kiyoshi relaxed his hands and flexed the stiffness out of them.

Eric's hand rested on his shoulder. "You okay?"

Kiyoshi sighed. "He's such an asshole."

Eric chuckled. "He always was."

"He was easier to deal with when I didn't have a girlfriend or now a fiancée. What crawled in his ass and chewed him up?"

"He's just jealous."

"Maybe," Kiyoshi said. Roger didn't seem like the commitment type, so why would he care at all?

Chapter 21

KIKO HUGGED THE PHONE to her ear. "I know it's exciting news, Mom. I haven't planned anything yet. It's all so overwhelming."

"This isn't the right time for a wedding. Winter's coming, and you have school to finish."

Of course Mom wouldn't be supportive. "I can handle it."

"Well, whatever you decide, your father and I will be there. After all, Yoshi saved our marriage."

Kiko cringed at the visual. "Thank you."

"But you're on your own with the expense. We don't have any spare cash to offer, which is why you should wait. Later on, we can help you with a big wedding."

"I don't want a big wedding," Kiko said in defiance. Was it true? Did she want all the sparkle and candles and fancy streamers?

"That's fine too. Whatever you want, dear. Good luck, and don't forget the handwritten invites."

Kiko pressed her lips thin. "I won't. 'Bye, Mom."

Kiko brought the phone back to the receiver and returned to the couch. Spread out on the coffee table before her, Kiko had stacks of bridal magazines on one side and school textbooks on the other side. She turned pages in a magazine, marveling at all the fancy options. She didn't know how much it was going to cost, but she had to start somewhere in figuring out a budget. The gardens and twinkling lights were beautiful, as was an evening ceremony, so softly lit and romantic. Kiko sighed.

Between her part-time job at the Gap, and Yoshi working late to find clients, a fancy wedding was clearly out of question.

A knock on her door had her setting down the magazine and rushing over. She wasn't getting much studying done anyway. Kiko pulled the door wide and grinned at the tall blond who'd spun her head when they met.

"Hi, short stuff."

"Eric, what brings you here?"

Yoshi's best friend, and now Kiko's, brought a bottle of wine. "An early wedding gift."

Kiko accepted it. "This is great, but I haven't planned anything. That's what I'm working on now, actually. Are you willing to help?"

Eric's brows lifted. "Help plan a wedding?"

"Yeah." Kiko grinned. Either he helped and she appreciated it, or he ran off and she had time to squeeze in some studying.

"Of course." Eric stepped inside, and she closed the door behind him.

"A single, successful, handsome man like you wants to help me plan my wedding to his best friend?" Kiko asked with playful disbelief.

Eric leaned in close. "I *am* the best man, and I told you I'm fascinating."

Kiko laughed. "And you're right."

"So what's first? Dress, venue, or music?"

Kiko rested a hand on her hip. "You'd go dress shopping with me?"

"I know a tailor."

Kiko didn't know what to think of that. "I was just about to call venues for prices."

"What are you looking for?"

"A garden. Something bright colored—bold greens with bright flowers, just like in the glossy magazine pages."

Eric smiled. "A bride who knows what she wants. I like it. My cousin owns the botanical garden on Layton. I could put in a call for you, secure whatever date you need."

"Do you know his rates for a Saturday night?"

"Probably around a grand."

Kiko's hopes sunk. She couldn't afford that, let alone all the other expenses. "Thanks for the info, but that's not going to work."

"No?" Eric asked, as if he really had no idea why not.

"I don't think our budget can swing that."

"My cousin owes me. I'm sure I can get you a day for free."

Kiko shook her head. "I couldn't ask that of you."

"Consider it my wedding gift," Eric said, hands rubbing her arms. His eyes glistened and he blinked rapidly.

"No way. I couldn't accept something like that. I'm serious, Eric. Please don't."

"Are you sure?"

"Positive."

"Okay then. What else can I help with?" Eric's eyes moved to the table. "Caught between studying and planning?"

"I should be studying, but my head's just in a flurry with the wedding."

Eric smiled. "How about you take a break from both?"

"For what?"

"There's something I want to show you. Your real wedding gift."

Those sparkles of nerves returned at his intense warmth. "You don't have to. I don't need anything."

"This...I think you do." Eric backed up and grabbed a magazine off the table. He rolled it up tight and handed it to her. "Take this."

Kiko did, amused and fascinated by whatever this was. Eric rolled a second for himself. "Swing at me."

"What?" Kiko laughed. "Are you serious?"

"I want you to know how to defend yourself."

"From what?" Kiko asked and looked at the magazine in her hand. "A rabid mosquito?"

"Just call it a hunch. Take a swing." Eric shifted his legs for better balance.

Not taking this seriously at all, Kiko swatted Eric on the upper arm. Eric twisted into her movement and pulled her close, trapping her against his chest. Kiko's eyes widened, and her heart thundered furiously. After an intense moment, he released her.

"Don't open yourself up like that. It gives the attacker plenty of space to work with. Keep your defensive arm up and ready to block." His hand lifted her elbow, positioning it.

"You want me to join your dojo? Fighting isn't my thing."

"Kendo isn't about fighting, and this, what I'm showing you, is about defense."

Kiko dropped her arms. "What's this about, really?"

"I promised I'd keep you safe. I can't be here all the time, and Yoshi's been away a lot, so you need to be able to take care of yourself."

"I can," Kiko said defensively.

"Do this for me, okay?" Eric was worried.

There was nothing for him to be so afraid of, but to make him feel better, Kiko raised her arms to strike. This time she stabbed him in the chest with the rolled magazine. "Gotcha."

Eric smiled. "Perfect. Using a moment of distraction in your favor is a great move."

"I know when to take advantage, and when not to." Kiko said, referring to his excessive gifts.

"That's smart. You'll make a great counselor soon."

"Only if I finish my last semester." Kiko made another move, but this time Eric expected it. He blocked. Next time, she'd choose a different area, less easily batted away.

"You still need a subject for your class project?"

Kiko smiled. "I do."

"When do we start?"

Kiko laughed. "Mr. Spreadsheets was serious?"

"I always keep my word," Eric said and reached out for a strike. Kiko hadn't expected the move, but she ducked. Eric's magazine grazed her shoulder. Being smaller was an advantage.

"Alright then," she said, straightening. "It's next semester. I'll let you know."

"Is there anything I need to do to prepare?"

"Just bring yourself."

"I think I can handle that." Eric struck again, but this time Kiko's attempt at a defense was off and the crisp paper got her in the cheek. "Oh!" Eric shouted and dropped the magazine. He collected her in his arms and assessed her face. "Are you okay? I didn't mean to get you in the face right before your wedding."

Kiko's hand touched her cheek. Their faces were close, and Kiko's eyes drifted to his lips. "It's nothing. Just a little sting. If any mark remains, I can cover it with makeup."

"I'm so sorry, Kiko. I should've anticipated—"

"It's not your fault," Kiko said, interrupting. "It just proves you're right. I don't have the defensive skills needed to dodge a magazine."

Eric's eyes met hers, and he brushed at her cheeks with his thumbs. "I'm so sorry."

Kiko gently lowered his hands. "I know you are. It's okay." The closeness was sending her heart wild. She'd pushed away her reaction to him, but now it was back. It had to be cold feet kicking up these feelings. Was Mom right? Was her wedding too soon? Was she too young for this?

She loved Yoshi.

She did.

"I have studying to do," Kiko said, unable to meet his gaze.

"I...I have somewhere to be," Eric said, backing toward the door. "If you need anything, anything at all, just give me a call. And I'm really sorry."

"It's okay, I told you." Kiko met him at the door. Eric being so close was a bad idea. She couldn't deny there was something between them. He was her friend—her best friend—and the wedding had her head spinning. "I'll give you a call if I need you. I promise."

Eric smiled. "See you later, Kiko."

Kiko closed the door as Eric left. She turned and leaned against it. She glanced at her school work and wedding magazines sprawled on the coffee table, but all she could see was Eric's face, feel his arms, and smell his scent.

Kiko pushed away from the door and picked up a bridal magazine.

Chapter 22

After much internal debate and research, Kiko still couldn't accept Eric's generous offer of a venue. The guilt would've been too much for her, and she'd explained to Yoshi they could only afford a courthouse wedding. Yoshi had been disappointed, wanting more for her, but she reasoned it wasn't the sparkly lights or flowers that mattered; it was him. Yoshi seemed convinced, and Kiko scheduled the first open slot during her winter break. She'd called her parents to invite them, and Kiko apologized for not handwriting the invitations. The chastising was minimal when Kiko explained after she graduated in the spring, she would scoop up an entry-level job while working her way toward her master's degree and license. Then they'd have the extra money to throw a proper party, but until then, Kiko was happy.

She was happy.

Kiko's maid of honor was a cousin she hadn't seen in a few years. They weren't close at all, and it was her mother's idea, but Kiko didn't mind.

She did, however, notice Eric standing off Yoshi's shoulder, and the look on his face. After Eric had brushed away the sting on her cheek, the cold feet hadn't eased.

When she'd read about the dreaded 'cold feet', she had no idea how real and strong it was.

The judge read the typical vows, and Kiko's stomach tied and pulled in knots. Yoshi's hands held hers, rubbing at her knuckles. He smiled, tears in his eyes. He looked dashing in his suit, and Kiko felt pretty in her lacy white gown, face smothered in a thin veil, and shoulders so puffy she couldn't see to either side of her. Both her mom and dad and Yoshi's adoptive parents attended as witnesses. As expected, Yoshi's birth mother, Sakura Anderson, didn't respond to the invite, but Yoshi said he was glad for it. He didn't want anything to do with her, and the invite was only out of obligation.

Kiko was lost inside Yoshi's dark brown eyes, and his knowing soft lips curved into a smile. His steady hands slid the wedding band up her ring finger. He was her protector, her rescuer, her lover, and she did love him.

She was happy.

Yoshi recited his lines after the judge, "I, Kiyoshi Takai, take you, Kiko Hada, my best friend, to be my wife—the kindest, smartest, and most beautiful woman I've ever met. I promise to encourage you to try new things, to inspire you to do your best, to comfort and protect you any and every time you need me. I pledge you my respect and trust, and I fully give myself to you in this marriage from now and forever, in good times and bad. I love you, and I love that you found your inner peace with me."

Tears welled in Kiko's eyes and she laughed. Yoshi spoke with confidence, as if he'd practiced for hours just to get it right. The emotion overwhelmed her, and she struggled to keep herself together. Her mom sniffled behind her.

Kiko's composure faltered—her breath hitching with a silent sob, and tears leaked down her face. She slipped the symbolic band onto her love's finger slowly. "I, Kiko Hada, take you, Yoshi Takai, to be my husband. To learn and grow with you as an equal partner in happiness and sorrow, strength and weakness, and all the hills and valleys we may encounter from today until we part the earth. With this ring, I thee wed."

The judge continued the ceremony, and Kiko's lips quavered, her composure threatening to break entirely, threatening to ruin their ceremony. Kiko glanced at Eric. He had tears streaming down his cheeks, and he didn't wipe them away. Kiko was thrilled a man as great as Eric Woodson was Yoshi's best friend. And hers too.

"And now," the judge said, "you may kiss the bride."

Yoshi planted a kiss on her lips, sealing their vows and distracting her. His arms embraced her, and a soothing French vanilla enveloped her. He'd been pounding the coffee to stay awake. Yoshi couldn't sleep last night. She didn't blame him. Her nerves kept her up too, but now it was over.

Their parents clapped and sniffled. His dad cheered. Kiko smiled with a wet face at all their support.

"The day we met in Blockbuster," Yoshi whispered in her ear, "was the happiest day of my life, but not anymore. I love you so much, Mrs. Takai."

The name felt so foreign on his lips. Her new identity was still her but part of him too. She never wanted to be without him, ever. "I love you, Yoshi."

Hand in hand, they faced their tiny audience, and both their moms took pictures—clicks, flashes, and plastic cranking sounds echoed through the courtroom. Kiko and Yoshi held hands and walked down the aisle.

Kiko was well aware Eric was behind them with her cousin.

"So, where are you taking me now?" After determining they couldn't afford a fancy wedding, Kiko had asked about squeezing in a small honeymoon before winter break ended, but Yoshi was tight-lipped about it.

"You'll see," he growled in her ear. That passionate fire burned in his eyes, and Kiko's body flushed with anticipation.

Kiko collected her fuzzy wrap to warm her against the Wisconsin winter outside. At the curb of the courthouse, a black limo waited for them, just like their engagement dinner. The driver was the same, even. Kiko smiled. Clouds of breath puffed in front of their faces while the driver held the door open for them to climb into the back. Kiko spun and waved out the back window. Yoshi did too, and more pictures were taken.

Kiko met Eric's gaze. He stood solemn, watching her by himself. He waved back as the car moved away from the curb and zipped down snowy roads. The heater blasted them, and the sun reflected off the shiny trim inside the limo. Yoshi opened a hidden compartment while Kiko admired her gold ring in the sunlight. Mrs. Kiyoshi Takai, the wife of a handsome man worthy of the magazines on their coffee table, a first-*dan* in kendo, and a climbing real estate agent. How did she get so lucky?

Yoshi passed her a glass of red wine, and Kiko's eyes widened in concern for her dress. Yoshi clinked his glass to hers while the car moved under them. "To you, to me, to us, together forever."

Kiko smiled, tears threatening again. They both sipped and managed not to spill when the limo hit a bump in the road. The limo pulled into a parking lot. Sensing no vehicular issues involving the bump, after all, Milwaukee's roads sucked, Kiko realized this was their honeymoon. She didn't need sandy beaches and extravagant tropical drinks; this was better.

Blockbuster.

Kiko laughed. "So, what are we going to rent?"

Indiana Jones and the Temple of Doom. We never finished it. I figure we should watch it at least once, straight through, with no distractions."

"We can try." Kiko chuckled.

"Pinkie promise?" Her silly husband held out his finger. She hooked her pinkie into it, and they each kissed their hands.

She was happy.

It took them three more tries to watch the movie all the way through. It was the hardest thing Kiko had ever done.

Chapter 23

Kiyoshi's eyes were glued to his big-screen television. It was game day, and after he and Kiko had explored their love all over this house, his team couldn't lose. Traditionally, he and Roger watched it together, but they hadn't been in contact since Roger's apology at the dojo. Since Eric tried to stop Kiyoshi, perhaps he'd overreacted in the locker room, but Kiyoshi wasn't in the mood to reach out regardless.

Kiko brought over a platter with chips and nacho cheese, setting it on the coffee table and turning away.

"Aren't you going to watch with me?" Kiyoshi asked. "I need my good luck charm."

Kiko's radiant smile sent his heart and his pants trembling. "I'll pop in here and there. I'm preparing for next semester."

"Class hasn't started yet."

"I've got my books, and I'm diving into the details of the upcoming class project. I still have to make a final decision on which research method I'm going to choose. Is that enough cheese?"

Kiyoshi beamed. "It is. Thank you."

Kiko went to the kitchen and returned with a cold can of Miller Lite and his wedding present from her: an awesomely bold yellow cheese hat. She wouldn't wear a matching one, but he grinned, because she was a sport about it.

"You are too perfect," he said, accepting the can while she placed the hat on his head.

Kiko winked at him and strode off into the second bedroom—her private office. After Kiyoshi had drummed up some new business, he put all his spare time into cleaning out that room. When they were roommates, it was supposed to be her bedroom, but now it was her personal study space. Clean carpeting, white walls, and a big picture window. Rows of bookshelves filled one wall, which she stacked with mostly textbooks and a few picture frames. Kiko did make their house a home.

Kiyoshi popped the top on his can and sipped while the opening announcements hammered through the house.

Kiko closed her office door.

Even though he was watching alone, his pulse jumped with excitement. He loved football and everything about it. This year, his team wouldn't make it to the playoffs even if they won this game, but since he wasn't a fair-weather fan, he didn't care. *Go Pack Go!*

Kiyoshi chugged the first can and set it on the table. The doorbell rang. He bounced out of his seat, humming with excitement, and opened the door. Roger's fluffy blond hair and reflective designer shades towered in the doorway. In his hands was a six pack of Miller Lite.

Kiyoshi's back stiffened. That was one way to kill a buzz. "What do you want?" Kiyoshi asked sharply.

"Ouch, man. Listen, I miss my buddy. I miss *us*. Yoshi, the game's starting, and I thought, for old time's sake, we could put our past behind us and move forward." Roger lifted the drinks.

Kiyoshi remembered well what his friend had told him. Roger had been unsupportive of him marrying Kiko, and because of it, Kiyoshi had no reason to allow Roger into his new married life. "I don't think so."

"I thought you'd say that." Roger smirked and leaned sideways on the front porch. He brought over—an end table?

"What's this?" Kiyoshi asked, guarded.

"The gift I promised. This is for Kiko to smash me in the head with. I wasn't joking, and this is even better than a slap." Roger's sincere eyes melted Kiyoshi's guarded wall. Perhaps his friend found some humanity after all.

Kiyoshi stepped aside and allowed Roger to enter. The blond carried the end table inside, and set it down in the living room. With a glance up at the screen, he set the six-pack on the coffee table. "Is she here? I want this weirdness over before kickoff."

Kiko popped out from the bedroom, and her face blanched. "Roger?"

Roger's eyes locked on Kiko.

A tingling sensation crawled up Kiyoshi's arms. "It's okay, honey," he said gently. "He's here to apologize and watch the game." Kiyoshi gestured to the table. "He even brought you an apology gift."

Kiko folded her arms over her chest. She didn't come any closer. "It was my mother's end table that was destroyed. Not mine."

Kiyoshi explained, "It's for you to smash him over the head. His way of saying he's sorry."

A look of horror crossed her face. "I am not hitting anyone with furniture."

"It's so you'll be even," Kiyoshi said with a shrug. The idea did seem a little dumb now, but it was too late. Kiyoshi dug in. If this was what needed to happen so all his favorite people could get along, he'd figure out how to make it happen. "This is Roger's way of squaring the two of you."

Roger nodded.

Kiko spun on her heels and went back to her office. The door slammed shut.

"Chicks, eh?" Roger said.

Kiyoshi narrowed his eyes at Roger. He could try to send his friend away, but kickoff started in less than a minute, and he didn't want to watch the game alone. "Beer?"

"Totally, man."

Kiyoshi tossed him a cold can from the fridge, and set the warm six-pack inside. They both sat next to each other on the couch and listened to the announcer. The Packers' kicker walked onto the field.

"You still have that old thing? Would've thought it brought bad memories," Roger said, pointing to Kiyoshi's family heirloom katana displayed above the fireplace mantle. Since finding out he wasn't a real Takai, it tainted his love for the sword, but it also reminded him of how much Kiko loved him and how much she was willing to do for him. And because of that, he loved the sword more than anything, except his wife.

"I'm keeping that forever. It's valuable."

"Saints this week." Roger sipped. "Packers are going to win. You can mark my words."

"That I can agree with." They had to. Kiyoshi's good luck charm was in the next room.

THE TELEVISION BECAME THE unsuspecting victim of booing, yelling, and flinging chips. At halftime, Kiko came out with her hands on her hips. "I'm trying to read. Can you guys keep it down a little?"

"It's game night. If you don't like it, go to the library," Roger said.

Kiko frowned. "It's not open over winter break. Want to try that again?"

"That's not our problem," Roger said.

"Excuse me?" Kiko asked and darted daggers at Kiyoshi.

"Roger, back off. Honey, we'll be quieter. We just got so frustrated with how it's going. Why don't you take a break? Come sit."

With glares at Roger, who ignored her, Kiko sat next to Kiyoshi, as far from Roger as she could. Kiyoshi loved having his wife cuddled up next to him, and she stayed for the commercials. Kiyoshi rubbed her thigh. "Beer, honey?"

"No, thanks." She stiffly patted his leg in return. "I can only read one page at a time, not two." Kiko glanced at Roger again, who munched away, staring at the screen. Kiyoshi sensed the tension in her body. He couldn't blame her for being uncomfortable near Roger. But the hulking blond had apologized, and Kiyoshi had already given him a second chance.

The game started back up with an energetic introduction from an announcer, who was clearly rooting for the Saints. A train of profanities tunneled out of Roger's mouth, and Kiko startled out of her skin. Kiyoshi brushed her trembling leg. Third quarter or not, his wife's comfort in her own home trumped buddies watching a game.

"Hey, Rodg," Kiyoshi said, elbowing his friend.

"What?" Roger said, eyes glued to the screen. "Oh! Did you see that shit? What the—?"

"Roger!"

"What?"

"I think we're going to call it an early night."

"Seriously? But it's the third quarter," Roger said with a hint of whine in his voice.

"If you don't like it, go to the sports bar," Kiko said with a smirk.

Roger's face twisted. Kiyoshi got up. "The Packers are losing anyway. Game over."

Kiko stood, and Kiyoshi hooked an arm around her shoulders, hugging her close and shielding her.

"Oh, I see. You want your privacy. Can't keep your hands off each other. It's okay. It's fine." Roger slammed down the rest of his can and dropped the empty. It clattered onto the coffee table, spraying droplets all over. He stood up, and his dark gaze on Kiko made her flinch in Kiyoshi's arms.

Kiyoshi had made a mistake letting him inside. "Roger, now please?" Kiyoshi remained polite. He didn't want Roger's anger to escalate.

"Sure. No problem," Roger said walking toward the door. "I see how you've changed, letting a woman boss you around. I dodged a bullet there. So long." Roger slammed the door behind him.

Kiko relaxed in his arms.

"I'm so sorry," Kiyoshi said. "He just showed up, and I didn't want to start a scene."

"I understand. You're always trying to do your best, and that makes you a good man. I love you."

Kiyoshi puffed his chest with pride, and his heart swelled with love.

"Can you please pick up those chips off the floor. Were you raised in a barn?" Kiko asked playfully.

"That was Roger."

"I believe you."

Kiyoshi bent down and collected the chips. Kiko joined him. "You don't have to..." Kiyoshi said.

"This is our house. We take care of it together."

"You know, Roger is probably going to come back at some point," Kiyoshi said.

"I figured as much. Until you cut him from your life for good."

"We should get a dog. You know, for security," Kiyoshi said.

"I'm not really a dog person," Kiko said. "But I wouldn't mind some cameras."

"Cameras only help the police after an incident already occurred. That doesn't make me feel reassured."

"I'll think of something," Kiko said. Her gaze lifted to his sword. He couldn't help but wonder what she thought just now.

Chapter 24

The blustery January winds meant real estate was in the slow season. Kiko had picked up extra hours over the holidays, but since she'd blocked out their honeymoon window, only scraps had been left. Things would be tight again for a while. The worries plaguing her meant she couldn't focus on reading ahead in her textbooks, and not having a chart of deadlines made studying even less motivating. What more meaningful preparation could she really accomplish in a few days?

Kiko tied her long dark hair back with a red paisley handkerchief and moved into the kitchen. She turned on a radio so she wouldn't feel quite so alone. She and Yoshi had their first Thanksgiving as a married couple right here. She'd made turkey at Yoshi's request. Kiko preferred steak, but that was harder to find and more expensive this time of year. She'd bought gravy in a jar, and cranberry sauce from a can. The usual fixings were easier—steamed broccoli, and mashed potatoes. Kiko was a toaster master, not a kitchen whiz.

Kiko stacked her lunch dishes in the sink and wiped down the counters.

She still wished they had others join them for the festivities, but Yoshi's parents were visiting friends who were dealing with severe medical issues. Kiko's parents traveled to extended family, and when they didn't extend the invite, Kiko nudged. Her mom said she and Yoshi needed their private time.

Yoshi had called Eric to join them. When they'd been on the phone, Kiko's heart skipped and her fingers fumbled her drink, spilling soda on the carpet. But Eric had to be across the country for the big meal, and he was regretfully sorry to have to miss it. But he'd promised to bring the T-day to them.

He hadn't.

Yoshi respectfully hadn't called Roger. Kiko would've rather been alone, freezing her tail off, trapped in a car, buried in snow, waiting for a rescue that wouldn't come. Yep, that existential dread would've been like rainbows and unicorns compared to a meal with Roger.

A ring at the front door startled her, and she dropped her washcloth. Mom and Dad just visited yesterday. They wouldn't be back already. Yoshi was at an open house. She wished him many new clients and a sale.

Kiko hoped the visitor was Eric. She opened the door wide and sucked in a breath, and not from a gust of winter winds smacking her in the face.

"Hi, Kiko. Uh, these are for you." Roger stood with his bulk filling the doorway and a bundle of flowers in his meaty fist.

"What are you doing here?" Kiko asked, blocking his way inside, not that her effort would do any good if he really wanted in.

He smiled. "I came to apologize for my behavior during the game. I don't know what is going on between us, but

I'm trying to make it right, and you're letting all the warm air out, so why don't you step aside so we can talk?"

"There's nothing between us, Roger. I don't want you to make anything right."

He stepped inside with a glint in his eye and closed the door behind him. "Then what do you want?"

Kiko wanted him to take a long walk off a short pier with pockets full of rocks, but that would only anger him. She glanced over her shoulder. How far was the phone? Could she reach it before he figured out what she was doing? Could she dial before he snatched it away? Kiko faced Roger and said firmly but politely, "I want you to leave me alone."

Roger brushed a lock of hair off her shoulder and admired her handkerchief. Images of his attack rippled through her, and her pulse quickened. "I think Yoshi would prefer us to get along. Don't you agree?"

"He'll be home soon. What do you think he'll say when he finds out you're in here when I don't want you to be?"

Roger chuckled. "Yoshi is my best friend. Has been for years. Since you signed on the dotted line with him, you get me too." He stepped closer. Thick fingers slid through her hair and Kiko flinched. "We can smooth all this out. I would be your best friend."

"What are you implying, Roger?" She didn't really want to know.

"Give me a little of what you give him. That sounds fair to me."

It was exactly what she'd feared. Kiko squeaked out, "I'm married."

"A little pen-to-paper doesn't mean anything."

Kiko stumbled away from him, heading toward the kitchen and the phone. Roger prowled closer. For every step she took backward, he took forward, like a child's game. The front door opened. Kiko wouldn't have noticed over the drone of the radio and her pounding heart in her ears, but the gust of icy wind caught her attention. Perfect timing.

The door closed, and Yoshi appeared over Roger's shoulder. "What's going on here?"

Kiko smiled. Her protector arrived. "Yoshi!" she said excitedly, so Yoshi wouldn't overreact.

Roger stopped his progress and gave her a dark warning glare. He said, brightening for his friend, "Yoshi, I was just waiting for you." He leaned close to Kiko, so close she could smell his acrid aftershave. Kiko trembled as Roger reached out...and opened the refrigerator. "Want a beer?" he called over. Roger grabbed a can of Miller Lite and tossed it through the air.

Yoshi caught it and traded worried glances with Kiko. "Is everything alright in here?"

"Totally chill, man. Just came over to see how you were doing." His broad smile made her shiver.

"I work during the day, as you should've been." Yoshi's voice was strained.

Kiko sidled away from Roger's immediate reach, slowly, so he didn't notice.

Roger shrugged. "I had a showing earlier today that took longer than usual, and I didn't want to drive across town to the office. How was the open house? Any bites?"

"A few." Yoshi's tone conveyed he thought Roger was full of shit. He met Kiko's gaze and picked up on her terrified body language. "I just got home. How about we continue this another time?"

Roger's hands balled into fists and after a beat, he relaxed. "I get it. She's something special, huh?" Roger smirked and sauntered toward the door.

Kiko exhaled in relief.

Yoshi followed on his heels, likely to lock up the second he left, but the brute stopped, blocking the exit. In a split second, Roger swung at Yoshi's head. Her husband ducked, and the hulking blond spun himself off balance. His weight tumbled into the end table right where he'd left it the other day. The wood furniture splintered into kindling under his weight. Roger growled and folded to his knees, assessing cuts and tears on his shoulder and wrists. He lumbered up to his full height with a snarl on his face. He pointed at Kiko. "You will be mine."

Kiko shrank under his finger.

"Get out of here, honey, now!" Yoshi yelled, but Roger still blocked the front door.

If she darted for the phone, Roger would stop her. If she darted for the back door, Yoshi would be left undefended. Yoshi was a good fighter, but he was no match for Roger's reach and weight. In strength and weakness, Kiko had vowed, she'd stay by Yoshi's side. While her husband kept Roger's focus, Kiko slid along the kitchen counter, inching her way to a weapon. She rolled open a drawer and gripped a steak knife.

Roger saw her. He shouted with such primal anger Kiko startled and her hand trembled. Roger charged at her, but Yoshi tripped him, and he landed on the floor. "Is that how this is going to go?" Roger snarled and flew back to his feet.

Chapter 25

Roger stood ready to launch between her and Yoshi.

"We want you to leave, Rodg. No one needs to get hurt. Just walk out." Yoshi pointed to the door. "Just go."

"Too late for that." Roger dodged Yoshi and dashed to the fireplace. The brute dislodged Yoshi's katana.

Kiko gasped and the blood drained from her body. Terror froze her feet.

Roger unsheathed the sword with an eerie glide of metal against leather, a smug snarl on his ugly face.

"You want her? You'll have to go through me," Yoshi warned.

"Be careful what you wish for," Roger said.

Kiko trembled and looked at the inadequate knife in her hand. Could she throw it so Yoshi would catch it without getting hurt? Would Roger intercept it and make this worse? She slipped the knife behind her back. With a two-foot blade, Roger charged a unarmed man.

Kiko screamed.

Yoshi, features serious and focused, parried the attack, but he took damage to his forearm. Roger was strong, but he wasn't agile. Kiko had to believe Yoshi's strengths could best Roger's weaknesses. But she had to do something. Clearing her head, Kiko darted to the phone and dialed emergency services. Roger spun, and the blade against the landline cord pulled the handset from her fingers. The cord wasn't severed.

"Do that again and you're both dead," Roger said on a snarl.

A muted voice came through the line, but Kiko didn't answer it.

Yoshi kept moving, and Kiko worried how long his stamina would maintain him with the leaking gashes. Swing after swing, block after parry after dodge. Yoshi's steam ran low and Roger panted, but still Kiko had no way to hand Yoshi a knife without getting herself taken or killed.

Just when all hope was lost, Roger stopped, breathing hard. Yoshi panted and folded to rest his hands on his thighs, but his tired eyes blazed with determination. Roger had finally blown off all his fury, and he'd come to his senses. That also meant in a couple days he'd return with another stupid gesture and a useless apology. This time, she wouldn't accept Roger back into their lives, no matter how much Yoshi reasoned. This was too far. Until then, she had another piece of broken furniture to clean up, but that was better than the alternative.

Kiko relaxed the death grip on the knife behind her back, but still, she didn't answer the phone laying on the floor.

With one swift strike, Roger reeled the katana back and impaled Yoshi straight through the chest.

Kiko blinked, gasped, and covered her open mouth with her hand.

Yoshi's lips parted to speak, but nothing came out. His eyes met hers, and his legs buckled. Yoshi collapsed with the sword protruding from his chest. He didn't move.

"I guess I had to go through you after all." Roger spat and turned to face her. "How about you, Kiko? Do you have any wishes? I'm in a granting kind of mood right now."

Kiko screamed. She screamed for her husband, screamed for the monster coming at her, and screamed until her lungs emptied. How could such a man exist? He wasn't a man at all. Just before Roger's meaty hand grabbed her, Kiko's senses returned. She had to stop this now, in a way Roger wouldn't expect, or Yoshi was going to die.

Kiko squeezed the hidden steak knife in her fist. Roger had already seen it, but after what he'd just done, he couldn't be thinking straight, or he was so sure of himself, he wouldn't care that she was armed. She remembered what Eric had taught her—use a distraction to make a move, keep a defensive arm ready, know when to use a situation to her advantage. Kiko was smaller than Roger, and she had to use that. It was the only chance she had.

"Roger, if I agree to anything you want, anything at all, will you stop this? Get Yoshi help?"

Roger slowed his approach. He assessed her arm lifted up by her face. The other was tucked behind her. "Anything at all?"

"Anything," Kiko said.

"Why would I agree to that when I can take whatever I want?" Roger asked.

Now was her chance. His immediate anger wasn't driving him. "Because isn't it more fun when I don't fight you? Wouldn't you like it more if I volunteered or if I *liked* it?"

Roger tilted his head.

Distracted.

Kiko bent at the knees and used her body weight to plunge the steak knife into his unsuspecting belly. She curled away, dodging any attempt to grab her, and she turned to face her attacker.

Roger blinked and looked down at the wound as if trying to process what just happened. "That counts as a point. I'm impressed Kiko. Nice try, but that's not good enough."

Roger grasped the blade handle and, furrowing his brows against the pain, he slipped the knife out of his abdomen. That was a mistake.

Blood sprayed. With murder in his eyes, Roger gripped the bloody knife in his hands.

The little voice from the phone stopped, but a police car's sirens approached from a distance.

Kiko backed away, trembling. She had nothing left to fight with. The monster wasn't human at all.

Roger shifted one thick leg to advance on her, but it gave out under the strain. With a groan of surprise, Roger dropped to his knees and then tipped over to the floor. The knife clattered against the linoleum and spun away from his hand. Blood pooled under him, filling the pattern in the flooring.

Satisfied she was safe, Kiko ran to Yoshi and collapsed at his side. "Yoshi?"

She was afraid to touch him. His eyes were blankly staring at the ceiling. The sword punctured his lung, and it very likely nicked his heart, but anatomy wasn't her specialty. "Help is on the way. Stay with me." Kiko pressed her fingers against her husband's throat, seeking a pulse and finding it weak and slow. But it was there. Kiko's eyes welled with tears, and her face heated with a pounding pressure. She swiped them away.

The ambulance wouldn't get here on time. In his final minutes to live, Kiko collected his hand in hers. "I love you. Yoshi, I love you so much. You stay with me, okay? I need you to know you saved me, and everything will be okay. You're going to be fine." Kiko ran her fingers through his gelled hair, not caring about the mess on her hands.

Yoshi's lips parted. Kiko smiled. "Yoshi!" He was still here. She leaned down and kissed his lips.

Her husband didn't kiss her back.

"Yoshi?"

Kiko touched his shoulder gently. "Yoshi?"

She felt for a pulse again.

There wasn't one. She pressed harder.

Nothing.

Kiko shook her head. "No. Yoshi, you come back to me. I need you."

Yoshi didn't blink. His lips didn't move.

"Yoshi!"

The radio played on, breaking the silence.

Kiko closed his eyelids and slid a fingertip along his parted lips. Roger had taken the best thing in the world from her before the ink dried on their marriage license. Her dad's values of being courageous and persistent were bullshit. Tears ran down her cheeks and sprinkled on his shirt. The sword, his symbol of the family who rejected him, hurt him for the last time. Kiko folded her face down to the floor, and she gave in to the body-wracking sobs.

The siren wails were indistinguishable from her own.

Chapter 26

The medics rolled Yoshi away, while the police questioned her up and down, and the paramedics looked her over. Kiko answered, nodded, and trembled, everything a blur. And when they all left, the silence returned, except for the drone of the radio, and now instead of her husband on the floor, dying to protect her, she was left with his blood to clean. As if she hadn't suffered enough. And she had Roger's blood to clean, as if he hadn't already ruined her life, now he stained the floor.

She had to pick up the pieces herself.

She was alone.

Kiko needed someone. She needed someone to hold her up before she collapsed.

Kiko darted for the landline phone and shut off the bubbly music on the radio. It was too much to bear. She dialed the only number she thought of.

"Hello?"

"Eric," Kiko breathed his name through sobs. "I...I can't."

"Can't what? Kiko, what happened?"

"I need you. Help me. Eric, please." Kiko dropped the phone, its weight unbearable.

"Kiko? Kiko! What happened? What's wrong? Kiko, talk to me! I'm coming over right now!" Eric's quiet voice reached her ears from the floor, but all Kiko could do was slide to the floor and sob.

WHEN THE FRONT DOOR opened, Kiko didn't notice.

When a hand gripped hers and lifted her to her feet, she couldn't think.

When arms pulled her against a firm chest, Kiko held on for dear life.

"I got you. What happened? Where's Yoshi?"

Kiko fisted Eric's shirt and pulled him closer. The heat of his body warming hers wasn't close enough. She tugged him closer. She pushed herself into his chest. Closer. Kiko needed to be closer. Tears wet his shirt.

"What happened?"

Kiko didn't know how long Eric held her like that, his strong arms enveloping her in comfort, keeping her on her feet. Squeezing her, reminding her there was someone here. Someone who would understand this feeling, this ache crushing her. The sobs dried, slowly, but Eric still held her.

She shifted back to face him.

"What happened, Kiko? What is all this?" He meant the blood. There was so much blood.

"Roger..."

"Oh, fuck, Kiko." Eric pulled her back against him, tipping his chin onto her head. "Tell me that's Roger's blood." Eric's voice broke. "Tell me, Kiko. Tell me."

"Some of it."

Eric's hands knotted in Kiko's hair. He sniffled. "Where's Yoshi?"

THE FUNERAL WAS A blur. Kiko didn't remember much of it except Yoshi wore the suit from their wedding and Eric held her hand. They were the last ones there, long after everyone else left.

"It wasn't supposed to be him," Kiko said.

"He saved you, but it cost him his life," Eric said. "He's happy he saved you."

"That's just it!" Kiko yelled.

"Whoa, what do you mean?" Eric said, turning her to face him.

"He didn't! He didn't save me! He died for nothing!" She pounded on Eric's chest with her fists.

"Of course he saved you." Eric stilled her furious fists, and he captured her gaze. "Otherwise I'd be standing here all alone in front of two caskets."

"He didn't save me," Kiko repeated. "You did."

"I wasn't there, Kiko, but trust me, I would've given anything to protect you and help Yoshi." Eric's eyes welled with tears.

"You didn't have to be there. You taught me…" Kiko brushed away tears, face twisting with sobs trying to break free. "You showed me what to do. If I didn't wait to do something, Yoshi would still be here."

Eric's fingers tipped her chin up. "It's Roger's fault Yoshi died, not yours. You must believe that. And I didn't save you."

"Yes, you did."

"You saved yourself, Kiko. It didn't matter what I said if you didn't act on it. I gave you the tools, but you used them. You're strong, Kiko, and you'll get through this. We'll get through this together."

DURING THE INVESTIGATION, THE police returned and took more evidence, and when she was cleared to begin the process of closing his estate, Yoshi's adoptive parents showed up to take a few possessions they wanted. The cold and callous birth mother, Sakura Anderson, never showed for the funeral, and she never sent her condolences. Kiko cried for him.

Yoshi's prized katana remained in police custody, and Kiko was grateful. She didn't want it or the memories attached to it, even if it was rightfully hers. Too much blood had been spilled for it and by it.

The worst part? The worst, most gut-wrenching part—Roger Meyer survived. He was charged with second-degree intentional homicide, and his trial was scheduled in a couple months.

Now what?

Somehow she needed to go to class tomorrow, and Yoshi's lease was ending in a month. The string of horrors was paralyzing. Kiko broke off a corner of a Pop-Tart, but she couldn't taste it. She was hungry, and she needed to eat, but she couldn't find the energy to do it. She'd lost weight, not that she had much to lose. Kiko sipped water and her eyes glazed over at the blood stains on the linoleum.

The doorbell rang.

Kiko rose and walked around the stains on her way over. Mindlessly, she realized Yoshi's security deposit was going to be confiscated if she couldn't get his stains out of the flooring. Her heart squeezed for him again.

Standing at the door, Kiko knew Roger was in jail, awaiting what had to be a guaranteed prison sentence. He wasn't here. He wasn't returning to finish her off. He was safely locked away. Despite all her reassurances, Kiko called out, "Who is it?"

"It's me."

Kiko recognized the voice. The only person who could make her smile. Kiko opened the door to Eric and his brilliant green eyes and shaggy blond hair, wearing a leather jacket and dark wash jeans. In his comforting hands, he carried plastic bags filled with Styrofoam containers. "I missed Thanksgiving, so I promised to bring it to you."

"Restaurant special?" Kiko asked, stomach grumbling.

"You know it."

Kiko moved aside, and Eric set the containers down next to her pastry. He looked at it with pity. "I swooped in to save the day, just on time it seems."

"Can we call this something else? I don't have anything to be thankful for this year."

Eric stopped unloading the bags and stepped around the table to face her. "Let me see if I can clear this up for you. You're healthy and alive. Roger's behind bars, so that makes you safe. You have one semester left before you graduate, and one day I'll call you 'doctor.'"

Eric's words always made her feel better. "You're forgetting something."

He smiled. "What's that?"

"Great friends."

Eric twitched and nodded. "Let's eat, shall we? I've got mashed potatoes, a bucket of gravy—"

"Bucket?" Kiko snorted a laugh.

Eric noticed. "A whole damned trough."

Kiko laughed again.

Eric returned to the bag. "Stuffing, pumpkin pie, cranberries, broccoli..."

"Oh, my favorite," Kiko said.

"Everyone loves pie."

"I meant the broccoli."

Eric rolled his eyes. "Of course you'd be the weirdo who loves broccoli."

"And you don't?"

"Not in the slightest."

"Then why did you buy it?"

"It was a package deal." Eric shrugged and lifted the last container. "And here's the turkey. Already off the bones and conveniently sliced up."

Kiko cringed.

"What? Does broccoli woman hate turkey?" Kiko nodded. "You can't be serious."

"I prefer steak."

"I don't have steak, but I can get some—"

"No," Kiko held out a hand. "Please don't. You've done more than enough already."

Eric stood, holding the last bag. "Then that makes this awkward."

"What?"

Eric fished in the bag and held out a framed collage of photographs. Kiko gripped it in her hands and gasped, unable to release her breath. Her vision turned watery. From their bowling night, Eric arranged the prints of the three of them. Some featured Yoshi and Eric together. Some were her and Yoshi. She swiped a tear away. And a few were her and Eric. She remembered him hugging her and she was a nervous wreck.

"That night is one of my happiest memories." Kiko squeezed Eric and sniffled. "Thank you so much. You have no idea how wonderful this is."

Eric drew back, and he smiled through his own tears. "I think I do." His face was so close to hers she could feel his body heat. His eyes roamed her lips and her heart sped up. Eric cleared his throat and said, "Let's eat."

Kiko nodded, sliding away from Eric and returning to the table. "The turkey's yours."

"What about the pie?"

"*That* you're sharing or risk losing a few fingers."

Eric laughed.

Chapter 27

Eric helped her clear the table. Dishes piled in the sink. While Kiko filled the basin with soapy water, Eric packed up the leftovers and set them in the refrigerator for her, except the turkey. He reached for a towel and took a dish from Kiko.

"That was great, Eric. Thank you so much."

He swiped the plate and stacked it into a drying rack. There weren't many to wash, since the meal came in disposable containers. Kiko scrubbed the next and handed it to Eric.

"You're welcome. It's the least I could do. Maybe next year we can cook together. I happen to know my way around a grill, and I'd be happy to make you a steak."

"In November?" Kiko cocked a brow at him.

"The best time."

"I look forward to it." Kiko handed him the next plate and he rinsed and dried it.

"Look, I hate to eat and run, but I do have to go," Eric said.

"Generously sharing a full meal with me doesn't qualify as 'eat and run'. Go. I can finish this."

"Are you sure?" he asked.

"I like to keep my hands busy, and right now, reading school texts isn't doing it for me."

Eric set down the towel and gave her a quick peck on the cheek.

Kiko's eyes widened.

"I'll see you later. If you need anything—"

"I'll call you," Kiko finished. She drained the water and rinsed her hands. "I chose my research method, and if you'd like to be my subject, I'd like to take you up on the offer."

"I'd love to. Just let me know when and where." Eric's lips lifted and his eyes sparkled with affection. He moved to touch her shoulder, but he didn't. After a silent beat, he went to the door.

Kiko followed him. "Turkey," she reminded him, seeing his empty hands. "I don't need that bird stinking up the fridge."

Eric laughed and retrieved the container. He lifted it in acknowledgement. "I'll make sure this doesn't go to waste." He paused. "'Bye, Kiko," he said.

"'Bye," she repeated softly. After closing the door behind him, she rummaged in her pitiful tool drawer for a hammer. Kiko wasn't getting the security deposit back anyway, so she didn't care about placing a hole in the drywall. Besides, she wanted to see Yoshi and Eric's smiling faces every day.

The doorbell rang.

Her eyes skimmed the table, expecting Eric had returned. "Did you forget something else?" she called through the door while she grasped the knob.

Eric didn't reply. Her hand stilled.

The doorbell rang again.

Kiko startled. Roger wasn't here. He wasn't returning to finish her off. He was safely locked away. It had become her mantra whenever the doorbell rang. She needed to change the sound it made. Kiko leaned into the peephole—that Eric had installed for her.

She didn't recognize the man. He wore a light trench coat and a wide brimmed hat—in the middle of winter.

"I need to speak with you, Kiko," a deep voice came from the shifty man.

She'd interviewed and discussed arrangements with so many people after Yoshi's murder, she didn't remember everyone. Kiko opened the door just enough to peek at him. "What do you want?"

The man removed his hat and smiled. He had wide jade green eyes, a clean-shaven jaw, a prominent brow, and celebrity-white teeth. Pretty faces didn't fool her, not even Roger's had. She stared, unimpressed by his attempt to be friendly.

His smile waned. "I have a job for you."

Kiko's brows lifted in surprise. Without Yoshi's commission, she needed a raise, and anything more distracting than sorting and stocking shelves would be welcome. She opened the door wide but stood resolute, arms crossed.

"Aren't you going to let me in?"

"I don't think so."

"What I'm about to tell you is something you should sit for. I will not hurt you."

"I've heard that before."

"Unlike Roger, I mean it." Just as she figured, he was another investigator or reporter. What kind of job offer did she have to sit for? Curious, Kiko stepped to the side, allowing him entrance. The stranger didn't walk around and browse her home; he just spun around and waited for her to close the door, blotting out winter's wrath.

At the click of the door latch, he clapped his hands together and gestured toward the couch. "Please have a seat. I need to get this all laid out for you and pop back to my lady Esther. She's handing out necklaces to help pirates fall in love. It's creative. I like it."

Kiko had no idea what that meant. She sat on the couch with her back ramrod straight.

He glanced around, lifted a chair from the kitchen table, spun it backward, and sat across from her in the living room.

"So, what's the job?" she asked, impatient to hear what he had to say.

"I'm down a staff member, and I've chosen you to work for me. Now, just to warn you, there is no pay or benefits, but I can assure you, with the right moves, you'll be *very* well off."

Kiko scoffed. "Why would I take a job for no money or benefits?" He was wasting her time.

"Because I can offer you the one thing no one else can—the time to heal. Working for me will bring you peace, and the reward at the end of your service is beyond any comprehension right now."

Kiko narrowed her eyes. "Contract work? Who are you?"

The handsome man in a trench coat chuckled. "That's the hardest part to believe." He looked out the window as if seeing something she couldn't. "There's a war out there, Kiko. Always has been, always will be." The stranger took a deep breath and stared her in the eyes. "My philosophy is a firm belief in free will. The act of one person, making even the most mundane of choices, can alter future events. It's the unpredictability of nature. It needs preservation."

"You're an environmentalist?" She arched a brow at him. "Is this a psychology study—nature versus nurture?"

"My compatriot believes all things should be orderly, what you may think of as 'utopia'. As you can imagine we don't get along well."

"Utopia sounds...good," Kiko said dryly.

The stranger sighed. "What year is it? Eighty-nine?"

"Nineteen eighty-eight. Why is that even a question? Are you okay? Do you need me to call someone?"

"Let me think. *Logan's Run*, or *The Time Machine*?" he asked.

Kiko frowned. Where was he going with this?

"The movies? Young people watch movies now, don't they? Have you seen either?"

Kiko shrugged her shoulders. She didn't watch many films, and science fiction wasn't her preference.

"Where a utopian society exists, there's always a catch. To make everyone behave in a way the leader decides is best, free will of the society is removed. When people discover the truth, there's an uprising. To prevent that kind of bloodshed, I prevent utopia. Makes sense?"

Kiko shifted in her seat, debating whether to call the police. The guy was a loon.

"One of my best curators has recently fulfilled her service, and now I need a replacement."

"Curator? For a museum? But environmental or psychological? Nothing you said makes any sense. Is there someone I should call? Is there someone missing you right now?" Kiko asked.

The stranger stood. His tone was clipped. "I'm trying to make this easier for you. I'm trying to explain in simple human terms what the situation is without terrifying you. I'm here to recruit you onto my team. But as a matter of principal, I want you to agree."

"You want me to agree to a job you aren't describing, for no pay or benefits, to take place somewhere you haven't mentioned. Sure, sign me up!" Kiko's sarcasm wasn't lost on the crazy stranger.

"You want it clear? I am Chaos. I am fighting a war against my brother, Order. I have an open position I call the Love Curator. Your job would be to match people through time that otherwise cannot meet. There is no pay, but I'm sure with time travel in the palm of your hand, you'll figure something out. The world is your oyster on this, although you may find difficulties with various cultures and language barriers. So, if you are comfortable, I am assigning you to the United States territory."

Kiko stood. "And that's as much crazy as I can handle for one day."

The stranger who called himself Chaos crossed his arms over his broad chest. "It's not a joke. In simpler terms, I need you to play Cupid to couples, and time is no barrier, but it does have restrictions. At the end of your contract, just as your predecessor, a new destiny awaits you."

Kiko shook her head. "I have dishes to put away."

Chaos sighed. She'd at least believe he called himself that. Wait until Eric heard about this. And he thought her love of broccoli was weird.

Chaos lifted a hand, and with the snap of his fingers, someone appeared in her living room.

Kiko screamed.

Roger Meyer, wearing jailhouse orange, shifted around, disoriented and confused. His wrists weren't in chains or handcuffs.

Kiko clambered back away from him, pulse pounding wildly in her ears. She glanced side to side, trying to unscramble her brain and do something. She ran for the drawer of steak knives. Kiko gripped one tight and aimed it at her nightmare.

"Kiko?" Roger tilted his head. "How did I get here?"

Kiko gasped at his voice. Her biggest fear came true. He was here. He was going to finish what he started. "D...Don't come near me." The knife trembled.

Chaos snapped his fingers again, and Roger disappeared.

Kiko spun in place, wild eyed and panting. "Where is he? What happened?"

"That was real," Chaos said. "This offer is real. Are we done playing games?"

Kiko's brain couldn't grasp what he just did or how. She stuttered, "I...I..."

"I'll give you an hour." Like Roger, he vanished.

Kiko blinked a few times, testing her vision. Chaos was gone, but the front door hadn't opened or closed. No footsteps.

Kiko shivered.

Did Eric spike the pie?

Chapter 28

SHE DIDN'T WANT TO accuse Eric of something he might not have done. He definitely did not spike the pumpkin pie. But not believing the vanishing act, Kiko poked her head outside. The blustery winter let itself be known, blowing stinging snowflakes into her eyes. Kiko squinted, focusing on the jagged sidewalks and the bus stop. No one waited outside today. Hardly any vehicle marks were in the snowy road.

Kiko closed the front door and shivered. Inside the furnace hissed, but the living room remained empty and cold. Kiko rubbed her arms. She figured hallucinating a strange being who brought out her worst nightmare and vanished into thin air was a side-effect of trauma. Kiko dried and put away her and Eric's dishes. With that done, she needed something to keep her mind off the stains still on the floors. She'd tried bleach and ammonia—not at the same time. She'd tried baking soda and water—at the same time, but nothing worked.

Her eyes shifted to the collage of photos Eric gifted her. She needed those smiling faces on her wall. Kiko went to her office and dug around, looking for any missed nails left behind by previous tenants. She had a photo frame to hang. One remained above the window. Kiko dragged a chair over and climbed up. Using the claw of the hammer, she dug it out and grinned.

"Got you."

She climbed back down and scanned the living room. Where was the perfect place to put them? Somewhere she'd see them all the time. Somewhere she'd find comfort.

Just outside her and Yoshi's bedroom door.

Kiko lifted the hammer over the nail, aimed, and swung.

"Answer?" the booming voice asked.

Kiko shrieked and the hammer smashed her thumb. She dropped it and spun, breath heaving and eyes wide. "You're not real... I imagined you. Go away!"

"Do I need to bring Mr. Meyer back in here?"

Kiko shook her head rapidly.

"Good. The offer is real, as am I. What is your answer?"

What if Kiko wasn't hallucinating? What if Chaos was telling the truth? For however long the contract was, she'd play Cupid to match couples through time, bringing them the happiness that she had for the little it lasted. But at least she had it at all. People were out there who never met their other halves. Could she give up her schooling, her career dream of counseling couples to bring them back to the state of happiness? Rather than being emotionally distant, the unmatched couples were physically distant.

Kiko still didn't believe in time travel, but she humored the strange man named Chaos, since he was in her living room, and Kiko had welcomed all forms of distraction since Yoshi's murder.

What did she have to lose?

Chaos had promised her a new destiny at the end. Maybe her dreams could take on a new form.

She had a job, one that paid. The choice he offered was to help people find true love. Or she could go back to refolding clothes at the Gap. Worded that way, the choice was easy. And if Chaos was actually some whack-job, she could run away.

"So what is your answer?" he asked.

"I have more questions."

Chaos nodded. "I suspected. Go ahead."

"How long is the contract for?" Kiko knew better than to sign on a dotted line without reading the fine print first. Length of contract was a big one.

"Until I say."

Kiko folded her arms across her chest. "I don't feel like squeezing onto airlines, traveling the continental U.S. after I turn sixty, so..." It was hyperbole, but hopefully he got the hint.

Chaos's brow furrowed. "You won't have an issue with aging, and you won't need a plane."

Kiko's eyes widened. "Wait, so, I become immortal?"

"Not like me." He crossed his thick arms over his chest. "But I will grant you a temporary reprieve from aging."

Kiko shook her head with a half-crazed snicker. Temporary immortality was the stuff of fantasy. This couldn't be real. The hallucinating was back again. Humoring her unusual hallucination, she asked, "How do I know where to go or what to do?"

"You'll know." His hard jade eyes peered at her with impatience. He wasn't convincing in the details of the job, but Kiko would take anything truly offering peace, and since she wasn't entirely sure she was in reality and not a bizarre dream, she said, "Well, okay."

"Are you agreeing to work for me?" He unfolded his arms.

"Sure, why not? What's the worst that could happen?" Kiko didn't actually want that question answered.

"I need you to say 'yes.'"

"Why?"

Chaos grumbled, "This is why I normally choose older people. Wisdom comes with age."

Kiko's hackles rose. "I'm not stupid. I'm being careful and asking everything I can to understand the situation and make a wise decision."

Chaos exhaled a sigh. "Just say 'yes.'"

"Yes." Kiko's voice was less sure than she planned. In the blink of an eye, Chaos disappeared again, leaving her alone in the cold house.

Kiko wrapped her arms around herself. She moved to the kitchen and wrote herself a note to call for a referral to a psychiatrist.

Then she scribbled it out.

Would having mental illness on her medical record block her from becoming a marriage and family counselor? As she stared at her handwriting, the letters blurred away. Visions flipped through her mind's eye like an open book with pages blowing in the wind. She saw the matches, where and when, like a faded image in front of her real sight. Kiko saw the trials and tribulations each lost soul must face to find their mate.

Kiko's hand tingled. She lifted it, flipped it, and saw nothing out of the ordinary. But she just knew how to use her ability to create a tunnel in time, passing one lover through to meet their destined other half. She saw their happily ever afters, and tears of empathy flooded her eyes.

KIKO TAKAI STOOD TALL, chin up, and she exhaled. That was a practice run. What year had she slipped into? She craned her neck around. Kiko stood on a sidewalk. Her first match was here, somewhere, and she debated the best way to approach him.

Chaos didn't hand her an instruction manual or anything. So she practiced lines to herself.

"Hi, I'm a time traveler here to match you with your true love." No, that was stupid and completely unbelievable.

"Hello, I'm new in town, and I need directions." Then she'd be told where to go, but when she returned, they'd think she was crazy.

"Good morning, would you like to buy some cookies?" Door slam.

Kiko needed a cover story, something believable, and something easily worn. Perhaps a college student working on a project. White lies were easier than bold-faced ones.

Voices of children reached her ears. Kiko turned, and two dark-haired siblings with bright blue eyes and tired smiles walked home from school with backpacks on their shoulders. When she saw their faces, their futures rushed across her new vision.

Siblings Mathew and April McCall.

She smiled knowing their endings, but tears filled her eyes at the pain and struggles they faced. Someday.

There was nothing for her to do now.

Kiko wasn't here for them.

It was not their time...yet.

Dear Reader,

Kiko gets her HEA at the end of the series, in **Years to Savor** (Matchmaker in Time Book 4). In the meantime, follow Kiko's final mission matching the employees of Animal Care of Wisconsin, beginning with April and Sam's story in **Seconds to Act (Matchmaker in Time Book 1)**.

As an indie author, I'm thrilled you decided to share your time with me, exploring the crazy worlds residing in my head and keeping me up at night. Your reviews are very important to me, so if you enjoyed this book, please consider leaving some stars for Kiko's backstory with Kiyoshi in **Minutes to Live (Matchmaker in Time Book 0.5)**.

If you found any typos or errors, I blame my cat. Rat her out at: support@stephanieflynn.com.

Thank you for your support!

Also By Stephanie Flynn

Find my catalog at StephanieFlynn.com

Immortal Protector series

0.5 Vampire's Distraction

1 Vampire's Deception

2 Vampire's Secret

3 Vampire's Promise

3.5 Elf Bound

4 Vampire's Demand

Immortal Protector Side Tales

Deer Holiday

Love Claws

Depths of the Heart

Matchmaker in Time series

0.5 Minutes to Live

1 Seconds to Act
2 Hours to Arrive
3 Days to Hide
4 Years to Savor

Pirates in Time series
1 Pirate's Prize
2 Pirate's Treasure
3 Pirate's Plunder

Time Travel Romance Shorts
Fateful Time
One Crazy Time

If you like your urban fantasy without the romance, too, check out Stephanie Flynn's other name, Marie Flynn!

About Stephanie Flynn

Stephanie Flynn writes action-packed paranormal romance filled with adventure, suspense, and danger. She lives in Michigan, USA, with her husband and kids, and she spends her writing time surrounded by a herd of normal cats who bat everything off her desk, including her coffee. Check out her website for more books: StephanieFlynn.com